The A

RYTE OF PASSAGE

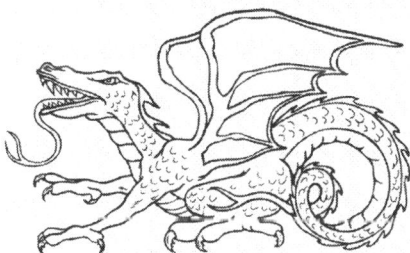

Titles available in The Afterland Chronicles Series (in reading order):
Ascension of the Whyte
Ryte of Passage

The Afterland Chronicles

RYTE OF PASSAGE

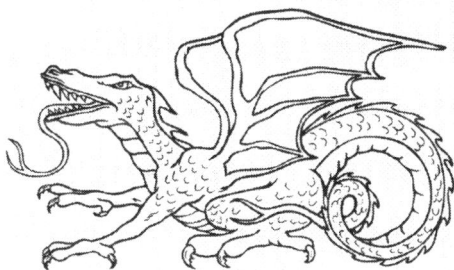

KAREN WRIGHTON

www.karenwrightonbooks.com

www.sleeplesspsyche.co.uk

Email: sleeplesspsyche@aol.com

Text Copyright © 2016 Karen Wrighton

Illustrations © 2016 Karen Wrighton

All Rights Reserved

ISBN-13: 978-1533059154

ISBN-10: 1533059152

For John, the love of my life, who read this first.

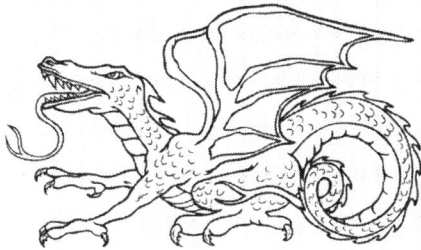

About the Author

Karen Wrighton was born in a small town in the English county of Staffordshire. Karen's first book, ASCENSION OF THE WHYTE, was the first of THE AFTERLAND CHRONICLES. RYTE OF PASSAGE is the second book in the series.
Karen has two daughters and lives in Norfolk, England with her husband, John.

"The power of words is constantly underestimated, with words you can heal, create, injure and even kill. Words justify our existence and define our humanity."

KAREN WRIGHTON

FIRST INCANTATIO

From knucker holes, thou must acquire,

Ice that stays the heat of fyre,

Keep it well in knucker's spew,

Until again, I heed to you.

This charm begins,

Though there are more,

Three to fashion that,

Which is cast, on four.

- CHAPTER ONE -

THE ELDER WITCH

Despite the crowd's tumultuous welcome, Rose could not ignore her growing sense of unease as she was escorted into the Elder Witch's dwelling. It was a gnarled, dynamic structure, each of its chambers hacked from the core of the giant ebony tree. Rose was led directly to its centre, into a small circular room with a dirt floor. The dimly lit hollow was crammed full of roughly made furniture, each piece peppered with a myriad of whorls, ridges and knots where branches had once sprung from the living wood.

A cauldron steamed and bubbled over a fire in the centre of the room. A loud crack broke the silence, Rose flinched as a burst of smoking embers shot out of the flames. The room smelled stagnant and musty like mouldy earth, and the fumes from the fire did little to improve matters. A jagged hole cut in the charred ceiling formed a pitifully ineffective chimney. The resulting pungent, choking haze leeched into Rose's eyes, causing them to smart and prickle.

The Elder Witch stood next to the fire with one hand outstretched, indicating a large wooden armchair draped in bearskins.

"Lady Rose, I appreciate you accepting my invitation," she said, turning briefly to the Twocast male who had escorted Rose in. "Thank you, Zac."

His dismissal evident, Zac, a well-built young man with a mass of unkempt dark hair, nodded and smiled. The white clay painted onto his face cracked, small fragments flaking off and floating to the ground like tiny desiccated snowflakes.

As Zac left the dingy, stuffy room, the Elder Witch eased herself into a sturdy looking wooden rocking chair, its twisted limbs rubbed smooth by many decades of use. The old woman could not conceal her obvious discomfort as she gingerly lowered herself into her seat. Rose sat on the bearskin-covered chair, feeling a pang of sympathy. Old bones... and this damp atmosphere cannot be helping.

Despite getting little sleep over the previous few days, Rose looked the epitome of youth and vitality; cheeks flushed and hair shimmering like spun silver in the firelight. In stark contrast, the Elder Witch's sparse white hair had long lost its lustre and her paper-thin skin had grown cracked and splintered by the passage of time. All the same, Rose found herself marvelling at the piercing clarity of the woman's bright violet eyes, and her delicate, angular bone structure, which gave her an ageless, timeless beauty that was surprisingly engaging.

"That was quite a performance you gave out there," said Elder, sounding impressed, though her eyes remained unreadable. "In all my years I cannot ever remember hearing such a rousing soliloquy. It would be difficult, if not impossible, to find anyone here who would argue with the power or the validity of your words."

She paused, leaning forward, eyes narrowing as her smile vanished.

"But that was your intent was it not, Rose the Whyte." Her words sliced through the air like shards of ice. "Is there no depth to your arrogance!"

Gripping the arms of the rocking chair, Elder's long bony fingers whitened.

"What gives you the right to speak to my people in that way?"

Rose felt a tingle as the hairs on her neck bristled. She recalled Vega describing the incidents that had ostensibly built the Elder Witch's evil reputation. The stories were mostly the product of rumour and gossip, and although now accepted as folklore they were almost certainly wildly exaggerated. Vega had cautioned her to be prudent just the same.

"I apologise, Elder," said Rose, smoothing the tremor from her voice. "Maybe it would have been more judicious for me to have spoken to you first, but..."

"Indeed," Elder's jaw tightened, her eyes brimming with fury. "It was I who watched over these people. For nigh on a thousand years, I kept them free from persecution, educated them, fed them and healed them when they were sick. Where were you and your kind then Rose of the Whyte? What gives you the right to take them from me now and lead them off to fight in your war? I have earned my ryte of passage with these people Lady Rose and you most certainly have not."

The old woman spat out the words with such venom that it ignited a furnace of fury within Rose. It's not my war. I didn't choose this, I didn't choose to lead anyone into battle. I don't have the luxury of choice.

Rose struggled to contain her emotions, two red blotches blazed high on her cheekbones. She gasped, gulping in a lungful of air; she'd been holding her breath. *Whatever is at the core of this woman's hatred is unlikely to be fixed by words alone, but I have to try.*

"I had no intention of taking your people from you Elder." Rose spoke the words softly, velvet, over cold, hard, steel. "because firstly, I was not aware that you owned these people, and secondly because I was expecting that, as their leader, you would accompany them. That aside, I am curious as to why you hate we ascendants with such passion."

"Oh, you are curious are you?" Elder's mouth twitched in amusement.

The woman's sudden levity seemed ominous to Rose, she felt her heart lurch in her chest.

Elder pitched backwards in her chair, its rockers hammering into the ground where the wood had cut two deep grooves from centuries of rocking. Ultimately, her rocking stilled, her eyes clouding, as she gazed, entranced, into the flames of the fire.

A menacing silence filled the room filling Rose with a deep sense of foreboding, the way the thick, sound deadening air and dark clouds, herald the approach of a great storm.

Each pop and crackle from the fire seemed dulled and yet magnified a thousand times. Rose shuffled in her seat.

"My parents were Whyte ascendants," Elder said abruptly, "though, of course, I never knew them."

Her voice was tinged with such melancholy that Rose felt an instant empathy for this woman who, like herself, had no memories of her family, but Rose was also confused. Surely both of them cannot have been Whyte ascendants.

"You are surprised by that Lady Rose?" she snapped, shooting Rose a look cold enough to freeze fyre. "You think that being landborn I am not worthy of being a Whyte ascendant?"

Her jaws were clamped together so tightly that every muscle in her face appeared clenched.

"You think me and my magic sullied because I am mortal. That I cannot possibly possess the powers of an ascendant because I did not arrive in a cubiculum?"

Elder's words were spoken with such bitterness that Rose began to doubt if she would ever be able to convince her to help them.

"No Elder, I assure you," Rose's throat had become parched and taut in her attempt at restraint, "that is not what I think at all."

The implications of Elder's revelation had started to register. Rose felt her chest tightening. It was as if the living walls of the small chamber had begun to grow inwards and would not stop until they had squeezed every breath from her body.

To have two ascendant parents was abhorrent, sacrilege. The chastity laws forbid Ascendants from bearing offspring. Even forming a romantic relationship with another ascendant is seen as a terrible crime resulting in enforced separation, exile and on occasions, long-term incarceration.

Rose met Elder's stubbornly accusing eyes. She gave an unconscious, disconsolate sigh. How can I hope to win her trust when, until now, every Ascendant in the Afterlands denounced her very existence?

At the oratory, the subject of landborn ascendants was rarely discussed and only then in huddled groups with hushed voices. As far as Rose was aware, no landborn ascendant had ever survived into adulthood. Looking at Elder now, she finally understood how grotesque this law was, a law that made abortion of landborn children mandatory.

"I had heard that one of your parents was an ascendant," said Rose steadily, "I was merely surprised to hear that they both were."

Elder arched one delicate feathery brow.

"I admit that I am somewhat surprised that you have been made aware of my parentage to any extent. You Ascendants so like to pretend that we do not exist."

Elder's body relaxed as she rocked. The thud, thud, thud of the rockers captured the silence, daring Rose to disturb their rhythm. A glimmer of emotion lit the old woman's eyes. Fear? Rose sensed fear, but also sadness and something else, anger? No, it was more than that. It was a dark, smouldering, soul consuming rage.

"My mother and father loved each other, but their love was unmentionable," her voice brimmed with bitterness. "I assume you are aware that ascendants are forbidden from forming romantic relationships?"

Rose nodded. "We were made aware of all of the edicts of the Afterlands, shortly after our induction at the oratory."

"I am sure you were," Elder sneered, "but did they tell you why?"

"To prevent our potens from being diluted," Rose's eyes locked onto Elder, as the woman arched a quizzical brow. Rose elaborated. "We were told that procreation results in our potens becoming divided. That it would be shared between ourselves and our children. If this were permitted to continue over generations, then with each generation our magical potens would diminish. The eventual outcome would be that we would lose our powers entirely or they would become so feeble as to be of little use. Our Cognito Magister, Lady Tesler called it ethnic dilution."

The Elder Witch roared with laughter, startling Rose for a second. Though her laughter had a surprisingly pleasant, musical quality to it that despite her anxiety, Rose found herself smiling.

"So that's how they do it," Elder's face was bright with amusement.

Watching her, Rose saw what her people must see, a striking woman who, like a craggy, mist covered mountain in the early morning sunlight, had the kind of charisma that was remarkably intoxicating.

"I often wondered how it was that all you young ascendants seemed so accepting of the situation," Elder said, with a chuckle. "I could never understand why there were so few illegitimate pregnancies. So many young, virile adolescents all of them thrown together, all fit and healthy and destined for productive and prosperous lives. Particularly as all of you are in possession of significant magical energy. Magic is such a potent aphrodisiac..."

Rose caught a flicker of something in Elder's wistful eyes and for a second, she felt peculiarly awkward.

"Did none of you ever think to question this law, Rose?" She asked, sounding disappointed. "Did you not feel the loss of this freedom, the freedom to procreate. To lie with someone you love, to cradle your child in your arms, or are you so young that as yet it holds little relevance?"

Rose flushed; she was finding the topic of conversation much too personal to share with a relative stranger. Besides, there were many more important things to discuss. The laws of chastity could wait until they had defeated Lord Ka.

"Truly, Elder I don't think any of us has ever given it a second thought," Rose struggled to hide her impatience, "not with everything else that has been happening. Lord Dux explained that we could fulfil our need to reproduce when we descended to Terra Coram, where there is no danger of ethnic dilution. We were encouraged us to see the members of our cells as our families and I suppose if I am honest, that we just accepted the laws and traditions as our norms."

"Ah... there it is," Elder, pointed a bony finger accusingly towards Rose. "Blind acceptance, the behaviour that enables discrimination, cruelty, corruption and victimisation to reign, and persuades fools to line up in gratitude to enjoy more of the same."

Rose frowned as insight delivered by Elder's words hit home. The more Rose discovered about the Afterlands, the more she realised how little she knew and how many lies she had so eagerly and unquestioningly swallowed.

"Enlighten me then," Said Rose. "Elucidate me as to what the oratory textbooks do not reveal, tell me the truth. Your truth Elder, the truth about your parents and how you came to be here, the truth about why you are so incensed."

"Ah… the truth," Elder gave a snort of disdain. "The truth, my dear Rose, is only ever an opinion, never a fact. Whereas a lie… A lie can make speaking the truth a terrorist act. If I tell you my truth Rose of the Whyte, will you rage against the lies that you have willingly consumed, or will you turn those beautiful eyes to the ground and follow the long walked path of those who travelled before you?"

Elder got to her feet and lifted two cups from a small table beside her chair. Grasping both in one hand, she took the ladle from the cauldron and filled them with a murky yellow-orange liquid.

"Maybe," Rose, was resolutely noncommittal, "I have learned not to make judgements without first obtaining all the relevant information," she paused briefly. "A Magister of mine once told me that time spent in the pursuit of knowledge was never futile. That reconnaissance often rewards you with immense power. We are in great need of such power now Elder."

The old woman straightened, hanging the ladle on its stand next to the fire.

"Sumac tea?" she said, seemingly impervious to Rose's plea for assistance.

Elder proffered the cup towards Rose.

"It's made from the seed heads of Staghorn Sumac. I hear it tastes like lemon, although unfortunately lemons are a luxury that I have yet to experience."

Rose took the cup in her hands. The brew smelled citrus sweet but looked unappetizing; a soup of brown flecks bobbing and diving like tiny insects.

"I added some honey for you," said Elder, "it makes the beverage more palatable."

"Thank you," Rose fought to keep her frustration from her voice.

As she lifted the cup to her mouth, the steamy, faintly sweet, acidic vapour warmed her face and left a dewy sheen on her skin. Her lips closed around the smooth wooden cup, and then she paused, waiting cautiously for the Elder Witch to take the first sip.

Seemingly amused by this, Elder lifted her cup in a mocking toast, before gulping down a substantial mouthful of the tea.

"Go ahead," she said, tilting her cup towards Rose, a wry smile twitching fleetingly at her lips. "It is entirely safe, and in spite of what you may have heard about me Lady Rose, I am not in the habit of poisoning young women, even if they do happen to be Whyte ascendants."

Her smile broadened as Rose took a sip and attempted unsuccessfully to conceal her distaste of the bitter orange liquid.

"I'm afraid, it is somewhat of an acquired taste," Elder chortled, "too sharp for you I expect. I should have added more honey, but, unfortunately, our honey is one of the few commodities that we can trade. Our bees feast on moonflower pollen, which grows only in the Ebony forest. It produces a thick, golden and particularly delicious variety of honey much prized by the Golds of Aurum. No doubt Vega is relieving us of the majority of our supplies as we speak."

"Oh, I doubt that very much," said Rose tersely, her cool slipping for an instant, " by now if any Golds are left at all, they will be too busy trying to stay alive to appreciate your honey."

"The Djinn have attacked Aurum?" Elder's voice raised an octave as if she had believed it absurd to imagine that the Djinn would even consider attacking the Golds.

"As we left a legion of Afreet were amassing over Aureus," said Rose, looking suddenly drained, "It is unlikely that the people of the capital would have either the time to flee or the means to fight them. Everyone who was there is probably dead, and it is only a matter of time before Ka and his army have control of all the major cities."

"I was not aware of that... " Elder paused briefly before appearing to come to a decision. "You must think me obstructive. That was not my intention. I apologise. From now on I will attempt to answer your questions honestly, Rose of the Whyte. Maybe then you will understand why, even now, I am reluctant to become involved in your war."

She took another mouthful of tea, sipping it slowly, her eyes never deviating from Rose's.

"During the Great Dragon War my mother and father were Whyte ascendants, both of them extremely powerful wizards," she gave a rueful sigh. "They fell in love, and I was the forbidden fruit of that love. Despite what you may have heard at the oratory, these things do happen, particularly during troubled times. Indeed, the realisation that you may never have the opportunity to experience one of life's most glorious joys may take a healthy, if illicit curiosity and transform it into an obsession. With all the senseless death, confusion and chaos of war, my conception was practically inevitable and relatively easy to conceal. My parents had little option but to leave me here with the Twocasts while they went off to fight their battles. I do not know whether they intended to return, but whatever their intentions, they never came back. All they left me was a single gift, by way of another, a few weeks after they departed."

"I am sure they would have returned if they could have," said Rose. *Is that why she hates Ascendants?* "Is that the reason you're reluctant..."

"It is why I do not wish to take any part in your battles," Elder's voice tightened. "My parents were killed in that war, ripped to pieces, along with every other Whyte in the Afterlands. Yet our world did not alter, it remains just as broken today as it was then. Look at how we live." She cast her eyes about the room. "We exist here in exile, in cold, damp hovels hewn from trees, our feet bare and blackened, our children undernourished and our bones aching from years of relentless toil. We eat only what we can forage or kill, in the winter we barely survive, and every year many of us do not. In my world, Rose of the Whyte, the truth, is that my people have to convince themselves every day that they are lucky if one of their children survives into adulthood, lucky. Weigh this against the sheltered, opulent lives of the Golds of Aurum. Then tell me which truth you prefer, tell me how this knowledge makes you feel Rose the Whyte. Does this information provide you with the power you crave?"

Rose struggled to meet her challenging glare. She felt the shame and remorse of her ancestors, of the four that resided within her, weighing her down, dragging her into a fathomless ocean of guilt. Like Elders parents, the four had given their lives believing they were fighting for freedom of their people. To make the Afterlands a safer and better place, and yet their demise seems only to have exposed and solidified the prejudice and disunity of its population.

"You heard what I said out there Elder," Rose swallowed hard as her eyes began to smart. *I can't blame her for not trusting me, I doubt I would either if I were her.* "I meant every word I said, Elder. You and your people have the power I crave, it is a power driven by discontent, injustice and hardship. People will readily fight for change when they have so little to lose."

Rose looked squarely, unblinking, into the doubt clouded eyes of the wise old woman, who, with her bright violet eyes, silver hair and fiery stubbornness, could have been family.

They sat in silence for some time. Rose struggled to find the right words to try to convince her, but they eluded her, there were no right words. The remorse she felt for the cruelty of her ancestors and of every ascendant who had gone before, flooded over her. Rose's pale, delicate hands clenched into a tight ball in her lap, the rose quartz crystal in her ring, pulsating, charged with magical energy, like a star primed to explode. Elder's gaze rested there for a while.

"What is it that you need from us?" Elder said.

Rose let out a gasp. She had been holding her breath again. Little by little the overwhelming sense of guilt and remorse began to evaporate, giving way to another sensation. She struggled to comprehend the jumble of emotions stirring within her. It was more than just relief she felt, more than gratitude even, it was pride, not in herself, but in the Elder Witch. This woman had so many reasons to hate Rose and everything she stood for, yet she sat here before her and offered her help, unconditionally. Gripped by a sudden compulsion Rose slid from her chair and fell to her knees at the feet of the old woman.

"No, I will not accept your help," Rose covered the witch's bony hands with her own. "Not before you have my apology. You deserve an apology Elder, and it is long overdue. On behalf of my ancestors and of all the ascendants I represent, I apologise. I am sorry that because of our failings you were abandoned here to live in exile. I cannot imagine how hard it has been for you. I cannot undo this great wrong Elder, no matter how much I may wish it, but if you allow me to try, I will do everything in my power to prevent it ever happening again."

Elder tilted Rose's chin until their eyes met and then she glanced away as a solitary tear slipped from the corner of one violet eye. Hurriedly she wiped it away before lifting her arms to Rose's shoulders and folding them about her in a warm embrace.

"Rose the Whyte," said Elder, "you have something about you that is quite enchanting. I cannot ever remember..."

She paused for a second as if musing on something, then shook her head, dismissing whatever thought had pervaded her consciousness.

Rose got to her feet, sobering as she stood before this woman who had the power to dash all of their plans.

"You asked me what I needed from you Elder," she said, "but it's not what I need from you that is important; it's that we need to do it together. We have to meet with the Ferrum resistance and key representatives from your community and quickly because it's likely that very shortly, if not already, Lord Ka will discover where we are and will attempt to eradicate us all."

Rose felt her body sway as a wave of fatigue washed over her. Although her mind was filled with thoughts of what may lay ahead, her body was trembling with exhaustion.

"I will do as you ask Rose of the Whyte," Elder smiled sympathetically, "on the condition that you get some rest. I will wake you as soon as everyone is ready, I promise."

Elder raised a hand, stifling Roses half-hearted attempt at protest.

"My dear child, you will be of no use to anyone if you do not have the strength even to stand," she said, "I've had a room prepared for you."

Rose hesitated. I've no time for sleep, I must prepare to lead an army and I have absolutely no idea how...

- CHAPTER TWO -

EL-ON-AH

The dark silhouette of a small dragon shadowed the first rays of the dawn sun as they sparked out from behind the distant Fyre Mountains. The animal's pearly grey scales glinted, dipped in morning gold. Frantically the creature flapped its tiny purple wings as if the doors of Erebus had opened up their fiery jaws and were about to engulf him. He plunged down, dipping erratically over the tree canopy of the Treymaneor forest, which skirted the Mapledale Plain. Hanging from the animal's feet was a slim, dark-robed, female. The pukis grunted, struggling to raise its mistress's feet above the needle-sharp foliage of the sticky, sweet-smelling pines.

As the full splendour of sun's rays finally emerged, they illuminated the robed figure of the female Blood ascendant. El-on-ah's long, red hair trailed out behind her like a cloak of crimson flames, blazing gold in the early morning sunlight.

The Blackfyre River stretched out before them like gigantic black python winding its way across the landscape. El-on-ah released the grip of her right hand and her body began to swing wildly in the air as she pointed towards the bank on the far side of the river.

"There Puk," she groaned, straining to hang on, "Over there."

She would not be able to hold on much longer. The pain in her arms had become unbearable, she was sure that they would give way at any moment and then she would plummet to the ground.

Swinging around, she grabbed the animal's hind leg, gasping as she caught sight of the scene below. Ferrum's Mapledale Plain was not as she had remembered; its once rustic beauty, the lush green prairie and quaint, wooden Ferrish homesteads were gone. They had been replaced by a vast area of scorched, barren earth and lines of blackened ashes that defiled the landscape like giant festering scars.

Realised immediately what must have transpired, El-on-ah could imagine the scene as Phlegon's army of winged Djinn pursued the Hydrargyrum refugees as they attempted to flee across the river to Ferrum. It was the only explanation for such absolute devastation.

As they descended, the pungent smell of ash mingled with the sweet, sickly aroma of charred flesh. The stench seemed to congeal into an unpalatable globule that lodged at the back of her throat, heralding her growing desire to vomit. El-on-ah gagged, and then spat it out onto the blackened grassland, now a grotesque necropolis littered with the seared twisted corpses of her people, many of them children. Doggedly, she pushed her emotions aside, as she had been taught to do, but she could not stop her heart from twisting in her chest. Another wave of nausea hit her and she felt relieved that it had been so long since her last meal. Her weakness embarrassed her. What is wrong with me... this is not the Blood way.

Once clear of the trees the exhausted Pukis lurched down steeply, flying so low over the river that El-on-ah's feet skimmed and bounced off its surface. The hem of her robe soaked through with water, weighing them down. The Pukis's tiny wings finally gave way, folding behind him like an inverted parasol and they plummeted down onto the muddy bank.

They lay still for a while, their strength returning painfully slowly to each quivering, exhausted limb. Finally, El-on-ah struggled to her feet, stumbling as she was pulled back down by her sodden, black robe.

The morning breeze was cool. Shivering, she clasped her arms around her body. Dragging each foot in turn from the squelching mire, she fought to climb the riverbank. Once she reached the dry rocky ground above the basin, she sat on a large boulder, took off her pumps and laid them out to dry in the sun.

Clasping her arms around her knees, she looked out over the charred landscape, only to be tormented by images of parents attempting to shield their infants from the deadly fyre of the Djinn. *They never stood a chance.* Burying her head in her hands, she sobbed.

After a while, Puk waddled up the bank, shaking the mud off his feet. Then, as if to confirm that his wings were still in working order, he opened them up, watching intently as he jiggled them about this way and that. Seemingly content, he cast a glance towards his mistress.

"Don't look at me like that!" El-on-ah's words were punctuated by sobs. "I know… I know… Bloods don't cry - only they do, I do…"

Muddy tears streaked her cheeks. Angrily, she wiped them away. *This is why they teach us not to feel.* She mumbled the Blood mantra under her breath, "logic makes you strong, emotion makes you weak, emotion makes you weak…"

Through blurry eyes, she regarded the broken landscape, peppered with hundreds of small black figures, the charred remains of her people. Then the scene before her faded, dissolving into a mist of faces; Rose, Tu-nek-ta, Che and Arjan. In her chest, her heart felt like lead. She knew that the genocide laid out there on the banks of Blackfyre was not the sole cause of her despair. No, it was because a few hours before, she had taken the life of another ascendant.

El-on-ah played the scene repeatedly in her head. She had been tasked with banishing Rose, casting the descent upon her and in doing so ensuring Lord Ka's triumph, but it had gone terribly wrong. She saw herself casting the spell, looking on helplessly as Arjan dived between them, throwing himself in front of Rose and taking the full force of her spell. Arjan, a young Gold ascendant, who had offered El-on-ah nothing but kindness and yet she repaid him by taking his life.

A buzzard squawked on the riverbank, flapping its wings aggressively as it fought another for a scrap of burnt flesh pulled from the corpse of a child. El-on-ah looked on with numb resignation. We do what we need to survive. I tried and I failed.

A fathomless gaping chasm was all that was left inside her now, as if someone had reached in, wrapped their hand around her heart and ripped it from her chest. Che and Tu-nek-ta were almost certainly dead and it was her fault.

El-on-ah pictured Che's rakishly beautiful face with its stubbornly determined jawline and recklessly sardonic smile. She clenched her numb, weak hands into fists, beating them down on the rock until they bled. *Stupid, stupid, stupid, I failed them, and I've failed Lord Ka...'*

The consequences of failing the Great Lord Ka El-on-ah knew only too well but, with a degree of dispassion of which any Blood would be proud, she realised that she no longer cared.

- CHAPTER THREE -

RESISTANCE

"Sorry Rose," Auriel's voice drifted into her consciousness as she felt a hand gently shaking her shoulder. "I wish I could let you sleep longer, but everyone's waiting. They're all so eager to meet you, and I wouldn't say they were a remarkably patient group of individuals."

Rose squinted, wondering where she was. The room smelled strangely familiar; musty sweet and earthy, a cross between dried herbs and meadow-fresh hay. Blurry eyes focused, adjusting to the light as they scrutinised the small circular room with its rough, axe-cut walls.

The midday sun streamed through an opening in the soot-blackened timber. This crudely fashioned chimney had forged the sunlight into a bright ribbon, a band of glittering light that danced with particles of dust, pollen and tiny hairs. The remains of a fire smouldered in the centre of the uncomfortably humid room and three straw-stuffed, hemp mattresses lay against the walls of the chamber. Straw, that's what she could smell.

Rose felt sweaty and uncomfortable. Tufts of damp hair were plastered to the skin of her forehead and a team of tiny miners were hammering inside her skull. Rubbing her eyes, Rose looked up into her friend's smiling face, which was framed by a mass of beautiful golden hair that floated around her like a halo of spun sugar. How does she always manage to look so perfect?

"Are you alright?" asked Auriel frowning, "because you look terrible."

Rose lifted herself up on one elbow. Yawning, she ran a hand through sleep-tangled hair.

"Thanks, friend," she shot Auriel a sleepy smile, "I can always rely on you to cheer me up..."

Auriel chuckled.

"They're all ready for you Rose," she repeated, continuing without taking a breath, "I've been sent to fetch you. They've prepared some food for the meeting. Apparently, every family donated something for us to eat or drink. If you want to wash, there's a bowl of water and some soapberries in the closet over there and if you need to do anything else... well I'll be happy to show you where the stink-holes are. No doubt, with such a gloriously descriptive name, you can guess what they are."

"It all sounds truly wonderful," she said, with an ironic smile. She stretched her arms above her head and her smile faltered, *every family donated something for us to eat or drink...*

"Auriel, these people have virtually nothing and yet they are still willing to share it with a group of strangers. Even though we belong to the very same ruling casts that have shunned and victimised them for thousands of years. One day I hope to repay them for their generosity."

Rose got up and attempted to wash using the oily, pungently fragrant soapberries. There was a small dish of them next to a wooden bucket filled with tepid water. However are you supposed to use these things?

Rose experimented by squashing them between her fingers. Eventually, she managed to work up enough lather to do an adequate job. Combing her hair through with her fingers, she glanced over towards Auriel, who was watching her intently and with barely concealed amusement.

"What's so funny?" Said Rose,

"Nothing at all," Auriel passed her a hand whittled wide-toothed comb that appeared to be made from some sort of polished bone. "It's just that they may not take you too seriously if you greeted them with your hair standing on end and adorned with bedstraw."

"Thanks," said Rose, quickly dragging the comb through her tangled locks. She paused, wrinkling her nose, "I think maybe it's time for you to introduce me to those stink-holes."

"Oh, it would be my pleasure," Auriel grinned. "I have only two pieces of advice; hold your breath and pee like a pukis." She laughed at Rose's confused expression. "All in one go and super fast."

Situated a few hundred yards further into the forest, away from the dwellings, were the aptly named stink holes. Rickety wooden cabins, fashioned from coarsely cut tree boughs, hovered precariously on tall stilts, which straddled a vast steaming, stinking bog.

The cesspool hummed with the buzzing of hundreds of fat green-bodied flies as they hopped from pile to pile in an attempt to distinguish the nutrient rich turds from more innocuous constituents of the peaty mire.

Rose gagged as she entered the shack. The foetid odour of stale urine and excrement filtered upwards through a hole in the centre of a roughly made bench. She covered her mouth and nose with her hand though it did little to quell the sickly stench.

Auriel was waiting for her on the path leading back to the Twocast settlement. A knowing and faintly amused smile pulled at the corner of Auriel's lips.

"I'm not sure whether it was a good move or not," said Auriel, "coming here before we eat."

Then, noticing the look on Rose's face, Auriel's smile rapidly vanished.

"How can people live like this?" Rose said, "It's little wonder that so many of their children die, there must be so much disease. How could we have ignored this? Surely, Lord Dux and the other Magisters must have known how these people lived. I am ashamed to be an ascendant, ashamed to have played any part in this."

"You have nothing to be ashamed of Rose," Auriel rested a hand on Rose's arm. "You are not responsible for any of this, none of us are."

Rose stared into the well-meaning, reassuring eyes of her friend and knew without any doubt, that Auriel was wrong. Just like that disgusting, fermenting cesspit, the shame of her ancestors bubbled up inside her, a stinking, putrid legacy of her ancestry.

"You are mistaken Auriel," Rose's jaw tightened, "I am responsible, we all are. Everyone who ever knew of this and did nothing, every ascendant that returned to these lands time after time and blindly accepted this normality. Even the Twocasts are not without blame. They should have raged and fought against this degradation and squalor. They should have marched to the high councils Aureus and Glynisfarne and demanded their right to equality and freedom. There are no innocents in these lands Auriel, save maybe for these children."

After walking back towards the settlement in solemn silence, Auriel led Rose to a large tree stump beside the Elder tree where Rose had spoken earlier that morning.

A cross-section cut from the trunk of an oak tree had been set on the stump. It had been hinged to form a circular door. Auriel pulled on the thick, looped rope handle, threaded through two holes in the wood, but it took both of their strength to yank it open. Beneath the door was a large shaft with a set of steps that descended deep into the musty earth.

Rose saw a flicker of candlelight at the bottom of the shaft. As she leant over to begin her descent a squall of thick, foul-smelling air rushed up from below. Reeking of leaf mould and damp soil, it carried with it a cargo of fine throat-clogging dust. Below, in the flickering candlelight, as her eyes began to adjust to the lack of light, she could see a dirt-walled passageway leading away from the bottom of the steps.

"What is this place?" asked Rose as she stepped onto the floor of the tunnel and ran her hands over a smooth wooden beam supporting the wall of the passageway. "This wood is too well finished to be the work of the Twocasts surely?"

"Correct," Auriel, placed her hand on the side of the tunnel wall. "I took the tour earlier. Apparently, these tunnels were originally constructed by the Glynisfarne Muds. We're in a section of the Ferrum Burrows. They were dug during the Dragon War as a means to evacuate the people of the city. Lord Alder said there were similar tunnels beneath most of the major cities. The majority, like these, have fallen into disuse, so the Twocasts made some adaptations. They store food in them over the winter and in the summer they serve as covered communal areas."

She bent forward lowering her voice even further.

"Though I've a suspicion that the Twocasts secretly use them to enter Glynisfarne and maybe do a bit of... scavenging," Auriel winked. "I can't say I blame them. I doubt there is nearly enough food around here during the winter. Given the choice between thieving or watching their children starve to death. Well, I know what I would choose."

Rose followed Auriel along a passageway lit by hundreds of candles that had been placed into small holes cut into the dirt walls. Deeper into the tunnel, the air became even more stale and the light from the candles began to dim and sputter.

"It's not much further now," said Auriel softly.

"Why are we whispering?" said Rose

"I don't know" Auriel giggled nervously, "It's almost like being in a Library, it just feels kind of appropriate. It is rather creepy down here don't you think?"

Their conversation was interrupted by the sound of muffled voices, interspersed with occasional bursts of laughter, coming from up ahead. A sudden swirl of cold air brushed past them, moving strands of Rose's hair across her face. Brushing them away, Rose walked towards the voices. Up ahead, the candlelight seemed to brighten again and the aroma of fresh bread, cheese and wild garlic, beckoned them on.

"Ah, good, you're here," Elder, strode purposefully along the passageway towards them.

In her right hand, she carried a long wooden staff, beautifully carved with delicately shaped rose briars. The head of the wand had been whittled into a knot and in it was set a large prism of vermarine quartz. The crystal glowed softly with a subtle green sheen.

Instantly Rose had the answer to something that had been puzzling her since they entered the Ebony Forest and she had witnessed the powerful cloak of enchantment cast by the Elder Witch. How was the Elder Witch able to cast such powerful magic without having access to a potens ring? Now all became clear. This crystal must work like their rings. It must be able to channel Elder's potens, magnifying the magical powers she inherited from her parents.

"Thank you, Lady Auriel," Elder waved her forward dismissively. "I will accompany Lady Rose into the Moot."

She led Rose into an enormous underground cavern. The chamber was teeming with people, many of whom Rose did not recognise.

"Welcome to The Moot," Elder spoke with evident pride, "we created this amphitheatre by widening a passageway and connecting two halls from the original Burrows."

Rose could see where they had made the modifications. There was a distinct contrast between the smooth, weathered, sawn timber supports of the original Burrows and the central chamber's roughly cut wooden struts, many with their tree bark still attached. The Twocasts had seemingly compensated for their lack of tunnel building skills by lining every inch of the wall of with timber.

In the centre of the room, Rose's attention was taken by a massive, roughly sanded, oak table laid with a selection of wooden bowls and platters. These were filled with chestnut bread, dried forest fruits, nuts, cured wild boar ham, honey, goat's cheese and butter. A Twocast male filled wooden goblets with a bright amber liquid.

"Moonflower Mead," said Elder, "One of our few luxuries."

The aroma of the food was enticing despite the accompanying odour of musty earth and stale air. Over a dozen people were seated at the table, many of whom Rose did not know. Deeply immersed in heated but well-humoured discussions, they rapidly quietened on noticing Rose's arrival.

"For those of you who have not yet made her acquaintance," Elder took Rose's hand and drew her forward. "I am pleasured to introduce you to Lady Rose, of the Whyte, who has requested that she speak with you today."

"Thank you, Elder," Rose extracted her hand from the witches grip. "Though I prefer, from this day that I am not addressed as Lady nor referred to as a Whyte."

Her words were met with silence. Rose sensed their uncertainty. She studied the colourful collection of individuals now eyeing her with unveiled curiosity. Rose's attention was briefly taken by Auriel as she sidled round the table to join the rest of Rose's cell. Ash met Rose's gaze with a wink and an encouraging grin. His bronzed muscular body and dark wavy hair set him apart from the rest of the cell, notably Lee, the group's pale, slim, scarlet-haired, Blood. Lee didn't appear to notice her, being preoccupied as usual, as he absentmindedly stroked his pharmacon loris. Sloley was perched happily on his shoulder purring like a content cat. Ash, Lee and Auriel stood slightly apart from the others with Vega, the Twocast tinker who had transported them all from Aureus in his wagon. These four were the only faces that Rose recognised; the others were strangers to her.

"So how then do you wish us to address you if I may be so bold to ask?" asked an elderly man with a nut-brown goatee.

"Rose," she said, "Rose, will do just fine."

Stepping forward from behind the table the man approached her. Dressed in the thick green robes of Ferrum, he wore the pin and potens ring of a Mud ascendant.

"Rose, may I introduce you to Lord Alder," Elder gestured gracefully towards the Mud ascendant, who, though not small, was somewhat dwarfed by Rose's willowy figure. "Lord Alder was Prime Councillor of the Ferrum High Council at Glynisfarne before the Afreet burned it to the ground. He now heads the Ferrum resistance."

Rose regarded the man's kind, weather-worn face, noticing the way his unruly brows framed gentle, glassy green eyes. Though his eyes exhibited only the merest hint of amusement, it was enough to cause them to crinkle slightly at the edges, instantly reminding her of Lord Dux. Rose's smile faded for a second as she remembered the Prima Magister and wondered once again whether he had managed to escape the attack on Aureus.

"Lord Alder, forgive me if I appear confrontational," said Rose, meeting his eyes, "but if I had my way, there would be no more Lords or Ladies, no more Muds, Bloods, Golds, Whytes and, most emphatically, no more Twocasts. We are about to battle against a foe that makes no such distinctions. Division only weakens us. We are Afterlanders and as such, each of us has an equal investment in the future of our world. Therefore, the value of each of us, native or Ascendant, can be judged only by what contribute to our quest to rid these lands of Lord Ka, his Ophites and the Djinn of Erebus. However we have more than one challenge ahead, we also need to build a better world for our people and unintentionally, Lord Ka has provided us with just the opportunity we need to rid ourselves of old prejudices and inequalities."

"Really!" An elegant willowy woman standing at the back of the room crossed her arms indignantly. "I have never heard such utter drivel, and this is what we have been waiting for. She is nothing but a naive child. Opportunity to rid ourselves of prejudice indeed. We need you to defeat Lord Ka Lady Rose, not reform our social order."

Rose sensed the eyes of the room resting on her and this woman with her high cheekbones, caramel skin and long, chestnut hair pulled into a tight knot at the nape of her neck. She wore the robes of a Mud Ascendant with a Memorix pin and she had the coldest, green eyes that Rose had ever seen.

"Anyone who is willing to risk their life for us," said Rose, "earns the right to be treated with respect and as an equal."

"You'll be expecting us to chop wood next," she spat, jerking her head towards Vega "while *they* run the High Council."

"Of course," Rose's brows arched over deep violet eyes that glinted ice. "I am no dictator. Indeed, I respect the freedom that each of you has by right, to choose to join me, or not, and that includes you… Lady…?"

"I am Lady Hazel... Mud Ascendant, Memorix and member of the Ferrum High Council and I see no reason to relinquish my status on the whim of a young novice who has been ascended to these lands for less time than a Rhodium summer."

Rose hesitated. If there was a prize for arrogance, there is no doubt about who would win it. Could everyone be thinking the same, though? Examining the faces of the strangers, she saw only uncertainty. The responsibility of it all felt suddenly overwhelming and the silence was suffocating.

Doubt clouded her mind, visiting her like an unwelcome but familiar friend. Lady Hazel is right. How can she, one so young, so inexperienced in the ways of this world, be the one destined to unite and lead these people to victory? She saw Auriel and Ash exchange an uneasy glance.

"Hazel," A tall athletically built Mud Ascendant broke the silence, taking her arm, his wavy shoulder length hair falling over one eye as he bent towards her. "actually I don't think that this is the time...."

"My dear Lord Elm," she snapped, "On the contrary, it's a perfect time, the girl..."

"Lady Hazel is right," Rose felt a sudden surge of strength rise inside her, driving the doubt from her mind and she knew that she could not afford to let this woman's words go unchallenged. Her voice hardened, "now is the perfect time to discuss your status - as you put it."

Rose's eyes narrowed. Few noticed their steely glint as they rested on Hazel or the piercing glare that should have broken her, shattered her into a million pieces, like a tree in an ice storm.

Ash noticed, though. Nudging Auriel's arm he moved his lips to her ear.

"Here she goes..."

Rose approached Lady Hazel, moving deliberately towards her until they were so close that Rose could feel the woman's heated breath on her skin.

"If you insist Lady Hazel, then we should, of course, consider your status..." Rose's voice was honey over shards of ice. "You flaunt your office as Councillor, and yet with the Glynisfarne Pyrus reduced to ash, that post is surely redundant."

Rose slowly began to circle her, examining the woman's immaculately pressed robes; the polished gold Memorix pin so carefully positioned over her left shoulder. Marvelling at Hazel's intricately dressed hair, she noticed, with some astonishment, that even her nails were polished and freshly manicured.

"I cannot argue with that fact that you are an Ascendant," said Rose, "but if Lord Ka prevails, then he will not hesitate to assimilate you, Lady Hazel, just as he did the other Ascendants who were foolish enough to believe that they were above this fate. Even his most loyal Ophites have not escaped this."

Rose levelled her eyes, meeting Hazel's indignant glare. She paused briefly as she sensed the gaze of everyone in the room resting upon her. Leaning forwards, Rose allowed her voice fall to a whisper.

"You boast of being a Memorix," Rose's fingers brushed the pin on Hazels shoulder, "and I would never wish to diminish the value of knowledge Lady Hazel, but knowledge without wisdom and insight is as useless as a book to a blind man. So how is your status looking now Lady Hazel, in this new world of ours?"

"And there it is..." Ash's lips hitched into a slanted smile, "expertly hooked, gutted and not a trace of blood in sight."

Standing next to them, Vega chuckled loudly, drawing disparaging glances from others in the room. Their disapproval only seemed to amuse him further.

"Aye, young Ash, that's what yer get when yer ignore rule number two so it is," his voice boomed out through a wide toothless grin as he nodded towards Rose with a mischievous wink, "never underestimate your opponent."

Hazel's lips parted to reply, but the words never came and her mouth, now redundant, hung open like a landed fish.

Ash snickered, turning to Vega, their faces lit with conspiratorial grins.

"I think I'd close that if I were her," he said, "a couple of those green-bodied flies were buzzing about down here earlier and you know where they've been dining..."

Their laughter had prompted a look of contempt from Hazel. However, their frivolity was cut short by three loud thuds as Elder banged the tip of her staff on the ground.

"We should move on and address the most pressing issues on the agenda. Lady...," she hesitated, faltering at the involuntary use of Rose's title. Casting an apologetic glance towards Rose, she corrected herself. "Rose asked to meet us all because she has something of importance that she needs to discuss with us. So, if those of you who have not already introduced yourself would do so, we can move on."

There were a few murmurs of agreement as everyone appeared to ignore Hazel's sullen pout and with a face like thunder, she slammed back into her seat, folding her arms and huffing like a petulant child.

"Allow me to do the introductions," said Alder, "I think I know everyone here."

Moving next to Rose, he turned to face the others, proceeding to point out each of them in turn.

"Rose, first let me introduce you to this strapping young officer here, Commander Linden," he indicated a gigantically framed, muscular young Mud dressed in a leather uniform with an embossed metal breastplate. "Linden was Commander of the Ferrum Lignum Vitae brigade at Glynisfarne. Be assured, there is little about the art of war that the Commander does not know. Though of course, like most of us his knowledge was mainly theoretical until recent events."

Linden clicked the heels of his boots, dipping his chin curtly as he slapped his right arm across his chest, fist clenched. Rose hesitated. *Is he saluting me?* She responded with a tentative nod.

"The Commander's companion, officer Blackthorn," Alder, indicated the young soldier at Linden's side "is also of the Lignum Vitae."

Blackthorn repeated the Lignum Vitae salute, Rose nodded again feeling somewhat intimidated as her tall, lithe frame became dwarfed by the bulk of the two men. Lifting her hand to her mouth she coughed, hiding a nervous giggle. *It appears I am in command of two gigantic soldiers.*

Alder went on, introducing a short, rotund man, who seemed to be in possession of more hair than face.

"Marshall Shadbush here was in charge of the Glynisfarne refugee camps, which housed the Hydrargyrum Bloods who fled from the Afreet. The Marshall was instrumental in not only their conception, but their construction and day to day running. Until they were attacked and destroyed... well, no need to dwell on that."

Shadbush's broad smile raised two ruddy cheeks out of his rather substantial and unruly beard. Alder turned towards a rakish Twocast male at the back of the room. White clay spiked his silver hair and etched three stripes across each tanned cheek.

"Tarik here teaches the young men and women of the village to hunt and defend themselves using a fascinating array of weapons made from the natural flora and fauna of the forest," said Alder, with evident admiration. "I have seen what they can do. Their blowpipes are virtually silent, as accurate as our arrows and even more deadly. I believe the darts are tipped with wolfsbane, although Tarik was somewhat evasive when I asked about it."

Tarik's lips twitched briefly as he bowed his head and approached Rose.

"T'is my honour to join you in your crusade, Rose of the Whyte."

"It is my honour," said Rose "to have you join us."

Lady Hazel snorted disdainfully.

"That's it then," Alder flicked a sharp sideways glance towards Hazel. "I think that you have met everyone now, except..."

He hesitated, searching the faces around him.

"Where is Lady Ro-eh-na?"

A woman's figure, silhouetted briefly in the candlelight, emerged tentatively from behind the Lignum Vitae officers.

"Ro-eh-na," Alder gestured for her to come forward, "I am sure that Rose would wish to meet you."

Slowly, the young female Blood Ascendant limped out into the light. Her tattered black robe, adorned with a single gold apis pin, indicated that she was a Metamorph. A wild mane of flame red hair billowed out from the hood of her cloak, which covered most her face.

Rose quelled a gasp as she caught sight of Ro-eh-na's hideously scarred face, its entire left side seared and distorted by the fyre of the Djinn.

Alder, moving quickly to Ro-eh-na's side, took her hand and guided her gently towards Rose. Ro-eh-na, dragging her left leg as she walked, attempted self-consciously to draw her cloak about her.

"Rose, it is my great pleasure to present Ro-eh-na, who not only managed to escape from Lord Ka and his Afreet but despite her injuries, she came directly to Glynisfarne to warn us of an impending attack," Alder's voice quivered. " Ro-eh-na, maybe more than any of us, has earned the right to be here today."

Ro-eh-na's dark, almond shaped eyes flicked nervously to the ground. Rose knew how hard this must be for her with all eyes now focussed on those terribly scarred features. She must be wishing the ground would open up and engulf her.

As Ro-eh-na approached, Rose tried to look beyond the scars. With those large almond eyes and elegant bone structure, Ro-eh-na must have been quite stunning before she was attacked. To go from stares of admiration to looks of horror. No wonder she is so reticent. Rose bridged the gap between them, placing her arms about Ro-eh-na's shoulders in a warm embrace.

"We owe you a great debt," said Rose, "If it were not for the information you provided we would not have left Aureus before the Afreet attacked. Your bravery saved our lives and likely the lives of many others. I am proud and exceptionally fortunate to have you at my side."

Rose kissed Ro-eh-na gently on each cheek, one smooth and soft; the other parched and cracked like old leather. Ro-eh-na's eyes brimmed, creasing as her lips drew into a lopsided smile, the left side of her face taught and unmoving like hardened wax.

"There is no need to thank me, Lady Rose," Ro-eh-na's voice was hoarse. "It is my greatest wish to serve you in any way that I can."

Once again, the conversation was halted by Elder, hammering her staff against the floor. Rose winced at the harsh sound. Someone was used to being in charge. It must be difficult for Elder to contemplate relinquishing her position after so long. With that in mind, Rose stepped back and gracefully gave way.

Elder's stance relaxed instantly, tension evaporated from her face and her expression softened markedly.

"Now that everyone is acquainted," Elder signalled for them to take their seats, "we had better get started. Rose..."

Elder moved to take her place at the table indicating that Rose should sit beside her. Rose gave Ro-eh-na's shoulder a reassuring squeeze and joined Elder at the table. The eclectic group of individuals took their places around her. Whytes, Bloods, Golds, Muds and Twocasts, representatives from all four corners of the Afterlands and all of them looking to Rose for direction.

A surge of panic leapt to her throat, twisting into a knot that barricaded her voice and tortured her with every swallow. As she cast her eyes over the faces before her, the Hornets of doubt returned, buzzing noisily in her head. *How can I be the Whyte from Eldwyn's prophecy? I'm no great wizard. I'm no different from Ash, Auriel or any of them. I haven't got a clue what to say. This is a terrible mistake.*

Everyone took their seats, except for herself and Officer Blackthorn, who stood guard at the entrance to the room. Apprehension imprisoned her words as their faces, bright with anticipation, turned towards her.

Rose felt as if she were about to vomit. That morning Rose had known what she would say to them all, but now it did not seem enough, nothing seemed enough. Who was she to instruct them?

Then, as another wave of panic threatened to engulf her, a natural calm descended and Rose knew that was no longer alone. Her wise, benevolent guardians had returned. *Take strength, Rose. Face your destiny... you are not alone, you are never alone...*

It had happened the same way when she had spoken to the crowd soon after they had arrived. Rose had felt the spirit of the four within her then. The four fragmented souls that made her who she was. Their strength drove her on. Though Rose had seen them only in her dreams, she often felt their presence and sometimes, like now, heard their voices. She sensed their arrival with the ease and certainly of a hound catching a scent. They were right, she was not alone, she was never alone. As before, her breathing began to calm and her heart ceased its frenzied beating.

"Thank you all for attending here at such short notice," Rose's voice displayed little of the fleeting panic that had overcome her only moments before. "We have much to discuss."

Rose cleared her throat; her mouth was dry. She lifted a wooden goblet of water from the table and took a long swallow, watching their eager faces over its brim as she did so. Placing the vessel back on the table, and with her anxiety finally quelled, the words came to her quickly, conjured from a script written by the wisdom of a thousand years.

"You are all, I assume, aware of the attack on Aureus," taking in their confirming nods Rose continued solemnly, "I expect that you know that, unfortunately, we were duped into transporting a group of traitors with us on our journey here, one of whom managed to escape. I am sure that I do not need to detail the implications of this."

Around the table, mutterings of acknowledgement were accompanied by gravely nodding heads.

"I do not wish to scupper any plans that the resistance may already have," said Rose, meeting Lord Alder's eyes across the table, "but under the circumstances I hope that you will agree that our priority must be to get everyone out of here and to safety. When El-on-ah tells Lord Ka what she knows it will not take them long to work out where we are, and Ka will not hesitate to order an attack. I do not doubt this for a second."

"Excuse me, Lady Rose," said Hazel "but as procurator of Eldwyn the Whyte's incantatio, surely you must agree that locating the components of his invocation has to be our priority. Eldwyn's spell is arguably the only way that we have any chance of defeating Lord Ka, how can you advise any other course of action?"

"As the procurator of Eldwyn's incantatio," Rose chose to ignore Hazel's confrontational use of her title, "I advise this course of action because locating the incantatio, though crucial, is not our only priority. If everyone in these lands is assimilated or killed then there will be no point in unifying the incantatio, there will be no one to save." Rose turned to Lord Alder, "I have thought long on this and I would like to suggest that we travel north to Rhodium. Lord Ka will not expect us to go there, especially at this time of year."

Hazel shot to her feet, her hands grabbing the edge of the table.

"North!" Her voice was raised and shrill, "we will not survive in the north, and Rhodium is nothing but a frozen wasteland crawling with Fae."

"My point precisely," said Rose, "Lord Ka will never think to look for us there. It's the perfect destination, and it will make the perfect stronghold. As far as we know Lord Ka and the majority of his forces remain in Cynnabar, almost as far south as is possible, without them getting their feet wet in Dragons Cove. By making Rhodium our base, we not only make our discovery less likely, but we also weaken the potential strength of any attack. The Afreet are creatures of fyre. It is unlikely that they would fare well in a land of freezing blizzards, invariably swathed in a blanket of snow and ice."

"Few of us would..." Lord Alder gave a small chuckle, "I think yours is a good plan Rose, but I am inclined to agree to some extent with Lady Hazel. I think it imperative that you continue your quest for the incantatio, it is likely our only hope of winning this war."

He paused, pulling thoughtfully on his goatee.

"May I suggest a compromise?" He said, "what if we split into two groups. My fellow Councillors, Elder and myself can lead the main party, with the object of forming a settlement in the north, perhaps at Isingwilde. It was the least damaged of the Rhodium cities and it is the furthest north. We are fortunate in that we have Marshall Shadbush with us; he is an expert in logistics. Under his guidance, I am sure that we could build a secure stronghold at Isingwilde. Then you and your companions would be free to seek out the incantatio."

"That sounds reasonable..." Rose hesitated. *If their help is to be effective, I must make them aware of my plans.* "However, initially, I will also be travelling north so we can journey together at least for a time. Have we a map?"

Commander Linden took a role of parchment from a leather container strapped around his torso. Unrolling it, he laid it out on the table in front of Rose, placing goblets and flagons of water at each corner.

The detailed, hand-drawn map of the Afterlands was colourfully illustrated. It outlined the four lands, their surrounding seas, islands and even the location and extent of the Ferrum Burrows. Rose traced her finger northwards from the Ebony Forest towards Winter Forest, and then west towards Kelpievale, Ferrum's principal fishing village. Finally, resting the tip of her forefinger on Ogin's Deep, the vast stretch of water, this marked the north-west border between Ferrum and Rhodium.

"If we use the cover of the forest to take us towards Ogin's Deep, we can split into two groups there. Your group can then travel east towards Winter Forest," Rose glanced up at Lord Alder, attempting to gauge his opinion. "The forest will give you cover until you reach the Rhodium border to the west of the Great Ice Wall. I'll go west into Kelpievale, where I'll cross Ogin's Deep into Rhodium."

There was a collective gasp from the group at the table.

Alder's eyes widened, "that area of Rhodium is crammed full of Knucker Holes, you can't..."

"I have no choice," said Rose, steadily.

"What does she mean she has no choice?" Lee turned to Ash, seemingly bemused. "One always has a choice."

"It must be where the incantatio is leading her," said Ash

"That may well be," said Lee, "but she still has a choice."

"No, she doesn't," Ash groaned in exasperation "not if she is to complete the spell and prevent us all from being wiped out."

"Indeed," Lee arched his brows, "but that is still a choice, and theoretically, at least, there may be more than one way of defeating Lord Ka."

Ash groaned loudly.

Elder pulled herself up with her staff. She stood stiffly, her reproachful, stony gaze falling on Ash and Lee, who immediately quietened.

"Sadly, I have to agree with Rose," Elder's voice was weary with resignation, "with our location almost certainly compromised, we have little choice but to relocate and Rose must be allowed to continue her quest. Rose, can we offer you any assistance?"

"Well, I believe this area of Rhodium is rather … inhospitable," said Rose with a wry smile. "So I will not ask anyone to accompany me. That said I would welcome anyone who does wish to join me."

"I," said Ro-eh-na as she got awkwardly to her feet.

Commander Linden's smile was full of admiration as he too stood.

"And I," he said, turning towards the officer in the doorway. "Blackthorn, you will accompany the main party north."

Blackthorn gave a brief nod of acquiescence.

Rose turned towards Ash, and the others. She sensed their uncertainty. They were all well aware of the reputation of knuckers, the great ice dragons that inhabited the Knucker Holes and briny waters of Knucker Bay. They had taken up two whole chapters in *'The Complete Anthology of Wild and Dangerous Beasts'* - required reading in their early Cognito classes.

"As members of my cell, I realise that you may feel that you have no choice but to accompany me. However, it is a perilous mission that I am attempting and I will not ask you to risk your lives."

"I'm with you Rose," Ash and Auriel spoke almost in unison as they moved to her side, leaving Lee looking slightly shell-shocked, with Sloley chattering away excitedly on his shoulder.

"What's up Lee?" Ash gave a mischievous wink. "You do have a choice you know. Everyone has a choice..."

"Well, of course, I should accompany you," Lee spluttered, "you will most certainly need an alchemist if you are reckless enough to go confronting knuckers."

"Err, I'd like t' come along w' yer" Vega cleared his throat, "Yea'll need some transport an' me wagon is yours if yer wish it?"

"While I appreciate your offer Vega, my friend," Rose took his rough, stubby hands into hers, "there are many children here and they have a long, arduous journey ahead of them. They'll need you and your wagon much more than we, and anyway, we'll be crossing Ogin's Deep."

"When do you plan to leave?" Commander Linden rolled up the map, placing it back into its holder.

"We should get on the road as quickly as we can," said Rose. *If it's not already too late.* "Elder, how long will it take your people to be ready?"

"A few hours. They have little to pack, but tomorrow we were to celebrate Beltane, the children will be very disappointed if we have to cancel the festival."

"Aye," said Vega "Tau an' Lily have been talking o' nothing else f' months."

"We can't risk waiting another day," said Rose, "the Afreet travel so fast. They could be here by morning. It would be very unwise to make the trek by day. We should leave tonight."

"Maybe we could bring the festival forward a day," Vega's bushy brows twitced as his face broke into an impish grin. "The women folk can sort the festival while the men ready to leave. The excitement o' the celebrations will get the wee ones good an' tired enough to sleep quietly on the journey. What d' ye say, Elder?"

"Aye," Elder nodded thoughtfully, "that's an excellent idea, Vega. You and Tarik should go and tell the heads of families to start preparations immediately. The festival will commence this afternroon, when the shadow of the great oak crosses the foot of the gathering tree."

"What will we do with our two spies?" Asked Linden, "Every second they are with us we risk them putting us all in greater jeopardy. I suggest we leave them here."

"No!" Rose said sharply, "the Afreet will make no distinction between them and us. They will burn the forest to the ground with Che and Tu-nek-ta in it. They may be misguided, but they are still Afterlanders. There has been enough killing. They come with us. We'll just have to ensure that they pose no threat."

Rose could see by the looks on their faces that they did not agree, but although she understood their reluctance to risk everything for the lives of two spies, she could stomach no more killing. Che and Tu-nek-ta were fighting for the rights of their people just as she was. Maybe that was even true of El-on-ah, though Rose was not ready to forgive that particular Blood ascendant, not when she had murdered Arjan. Unconsciously her eyes drifted to Lee. He, like El-on-ah, was a Blood Alchemist. He made decisions using the same cool, detached logic. It's what made them so good at what they did.

Picking a grape from the display on the table, Lee tossed it to the loris perched on his shoulder. There was so much tenderness in the way that Lee handled the little creature, they had not been parted since that first day in the Alchemy classroom. Maybe, Bloods were not all as cold hearted, as they would have everyone think.

As she watched them, Rose had the spark of an idea.

"Lee, Could you and Sloley cook up an Oblitus potion?"

"It's possible," Lee raised his brows and grinned.

Lee rarely smiled, but in response to the challenge of brewing some convoluted charm or potion, he became positively euphoric.

"It has been a warm spring, so the ephedra may be ripe enough to harvest and Sloley should have no trouble locating some if there are any about. The rest of the ingredients are commonplace, but Oblitus is not permanent Rose, their memories will return."

"Then you should make enough to for a few weeks regular dosage, Elder can have someone slip it into their food," said Rose. "We cannot risk them giving away our position, or our plans and they'll be no threat to anyone if we remove their memory."

- CHAPTER FOUR -

FYRE MEISTER

From the balcony of his chambers in the Cynnabar Pyrus, Lord Ka looked out to the east over the steaming dark waters of Loch Drac, washed blood red by the dawn sun. Irritated, sensing that he was no longer alone, Ka turned and walked back into the room. Passing the large ornate wall mirror, he caught sight of his reflection. The image unnerved him.

The eyes that gazed back at him were as he remembered, but their setting, that grotesque mask of a face reflected in the mirror, was that of a stranger. Since the assimilation, he wore the features of a djinn, the image of Fyre Meister Phlegon.

Ka had been expecting Phlegon's attack. Indeed, he had been counting on it to use his reverse assimilation charm. This was how he was able to take the place of his enemy. However, he had not anticipated the charms mutilating effect. Now, trapped for eternity in this hideous reptilian body, he would have to maintain this charade until he replaced every one of the djinn's prime circle with his Ophite followers. Only then would he have the power to control the Afreet army, not as Meister Phlegon, but as Lord Ka-ek-tal the one true ruler of the Afterlands.

He forced a lipless smile in greeting to the female djinn. She moved beside him to gaze at their reflections in the mirror. As his face contorted, his red-scaled skin twitched, pulling tight over his new reptilian features. Two spindle-shaped breathing holes at the centre of his face flared open as he inhaled deeply before spinning round to confront the Fyre Miester's consort.

Having Shevanna around disturbed him. She, like all djinn was hot blooded, a volcano of emotion primed to explode without a moments notice. She was unpredictable, and that made her dangerous. When she was around, he was almost constantly on edge. He would have to do something about her, and rapidly.

Everything else gone well. Progress had been rapid and without incident. Most of the prime circle had been assimilated and replaced by his Ophite ascendants. Almost Phlegon's entire inner circle, like he, appeared on the outside to be a djinn, but their bodies were merely vessels for the consciousness of his followers.

Shevanna, however, had repeatedly resisted his attempts to persuade her to assimilate any of the remaining imprisoned Ophites. Therefore, Ka had been unable to replace her. Consequently, Shevanna continued to be a significant threat.

Ka sensed her mistrust in him. She suspected that something was not right, he was convinced of it. This thought plagued him now, if he was right, then why had she not acted against him. Maybe she doubted her instincts? Shevanna would not risk challenging Phlegon if she were not certain. Until she was replaced, he would have to convince her every day, that beneath this altered shell of a body resided the essence of Fyre Meister Phlegon and that he remained in full control. All of his plans and all of their lives depended on it.

"Sheeva," Ka used Phlegon's pet name for her.

Taking her face in his hands, he planted a kiss lightly on her forehead as she bowed her head briefly in deference to his status.

"I see that you have discovered Aurum lace... it is most becoming my dear."

Kissing her filled him with revulsion. Her reptilian skin disgusted him, as did that wide lipless mouth and those cold serpentine eyes. The skin of female djinn released powerful pheromones, their sulphurous stench made him gag. He drew back from her on the pretext of admiring her robe. She struck a pose for him. The long, tightly fitting ivory gown barely covered her voluptuous red-scaled body. A slit ran from the top of the skirt, down one shapely thigh to her ankle. Shevanna's long black hair flowed loosely around her shoulders.

"I am pleased that you approve, Meister," she said, dipping her chin demurely to one side and allowing the strap of her gown to slide seductively down one shoulder. "I had hoped to tempt you out of your solitude my liege, for it seems that since we left our realm, your passion for me had cooled along with the climate. You needed no such incentives in Erebus... Fyre Meister."

Her mood appeared playful and teasing as she moved towards him. Reaching out, she rested her hands lightly his shoulders, sliding them slowly down onto his chest.

Doubting that this advance was as spontaneous as she would have it appear, Ka decided that it was yet another one of her tests. He had been subjected to a few them over the past few days. They were designed to stir the hot-blooded Djinn into action or, conversely, to uncover the cold-blooded imposter holding hostage to his body.

Blood ascendants were celibate, passionless beings and as such, Ka was indifferent to her advances. If Shevanna was attempting to discover whether it was Phlegon or he, who had completed the assimilation process, then this was an ingenious way to distinguish between them. If he did not take great care, his deception would be uncovered.

Moving her body closer, she traced the contours of his waist with her fingertips, allowing them to slip downwards and linger provocatively over his hips. Ka's body tensed. However, unnervingly, he sensed his body stirring. He gasped, as his limbs began to react, seemingly autonomously his arms reached down, lifting Shevanna effortlessly, holding her tight against his chest.

Her startled expression seemed to trigger something within him. An urge possessed him, driving his body into a frenzied, instinctive response. He hurled Shevanna onto his bed, throwing himself upon her, pinning her down and striking her fiercely across the face. Then he ripped the flimsy gown from her body.

"Phlegon," Shevanna's voice was hoarse and thick with passion, "my liege, I was afraid I had lost you..."

Stifling her words with his lips, he forced open her mouth. His mind was whirling, intoxicated and as if in a dream, he surveyed the scene like a dispassionate observer.

He fought in vain to control his actions. This body was no longer his and yet he was conscious of every foreign sensation that coursed through it. He felt their familiar presence, but they were lost, like a distant memory that resisted his recall.

His heart pounded furiously as his limbs moved purposefully, without his direction as if some malevolent, omniscient puppet master directed each movement. His breath caught in his throat, *Phlegon*. He recognised his new vulnerability, and it filled him with terror, but his fear began to ebb as he found himself savouring these exotic sensations and sadistically revelling in their intense eroticism.

His terror now intermingled with a myriad of alien emotions as he moved rhythmically and in harmonious autonomy, with Shevanna's body. Her limbs were now so tightly entwined with his own that he could no longer distinguish between them. Soon he could reason no longer, his senses owned him as their bodies writhed and arched together.

"No!" Ka could not stop, and what was more, he did not wish to.

A small whimper escaped him before the intensity of what he was feeling erupted, filling his mind with an electrifying buzz, drowning his thoughts and smothering his consciousness. Finally, he crumpled onto her, humiliated, reduced to nothing more than a vessel for Phlegon's passion.

Ka awoke to the sound of light knocking on the door of his chambers. Shevanna lay sleeping beside him. Her form repulsed him though he could not put the experience of the previous evening out of his mind and as he recalled their lovemaking; his body began to stir once more. Pulling on his robe, he left the bedchamber feeling strangely conflicted, as a once stung bear presented with a hive full of honey. This cannot happen again.

"Enter," he said, taking a seat at his breakfast table.

Afreet Commander Zelron entered the room, followed by two officers escorting a young, female Blood ascendant. Ka winced at the jarring sound of their marching feet, leather uniforms, and armour.

He was surprised to see El-on-ah though he took great care not to react. That she was here before him was an ominous sign. His mind filled with questions he could not voice. El-on-ah had proved her dedication on more than one occasion. So what has prompted her to come here and put them all in danger? His jaw tightened, as he struggled to maintain his composure.

"Commander," said Ka with an air of mocking amusement, "I see that you have recaptured the Blood ascendant that you once so carelessly misplaced. Did you also locate the Pukis who aided her?"

"No, Fyre Meister," Zelron motioned towards the officers, indicating that they should wait in the doorway. "The woman was alone when she approached the guards at the gates of the city. She insists that she has information regarding an imminent threat that you would wish to hear without delay."

Casually, Ka lifted a peach from the platter of fruit on the table before him. *What game is she playing?*

Sniffing the fruit briefly, he took a large bite from its sweet ripe flesh. The juice seeped from the sides of his lipless mouth and trickled down his chin. It's syrupy fragrance filled the air. Wiping the sticky juice from his face he studied El-on-ah carefully, marvelling at her apparent composure. Surely, she must realise how precarious her position was. *What is she doing here?*

Ka motioned the guards to bring her forward. As they did, they remained close, maintaining a firm grip on El-on-ah's arms and the hilts of their swords.

"Speak," Ka had little choice but to play along with whatever plan she had hatched.

In an instant, El-on-ah twisted, pulling free of the Afreet officers she lurched towards him. The officers drew their swords.

Ka raised a hand. "No, I wish to hear what the Blood has to say."

El-on-ah's knuckles whitened as she grasped at the edge of the table in front of him.

"Meister Phlegon," El-on-ah addressed him with an air of calm control that Ka was sure she could not be feeling.

Her eyes betrayed little and yet he sensed her antagonism though her cool wavered only briefly as she shot a nervous glance in Zelron's direction.

A smile tugged at the side of his mouth. *She is far from composed, yet she hides it so well.* The rigidity of his new orifice hid his fleeting expression of admiration from her.

Curious as to how she intended to get herself out of this precarious position Ka studied her carefully. *Did she intend to unmask him? If so, was not overly concerned, it was unlikely that any of the djinns would take the word of a Blood Ascendant over his and he could order her assimilation if necessary. Few Djinn would have the gall to question his authority.* El-on-ah, however, had little hope of escape, she had sealed her fate the moment she entered the city. *So why had she come?* He felt his impatience growing.

"Meister Phlegon, you assimilated my Lord Ka and so have access to his memories," El-on-ah paused for a second. "So you will recognise me as Lady El-on-ah, Blood Alchemist and Lord Ka's successor as leader of the Ophites. You will also know that we Ophites have sworn an allegiance to the Djinn of Erebus and are therefore no threat to you. Indeed, we wish to become your allies."

Ka's tight-scaled brow creased, his black eyes shot a piercing look towards El-on-ah. *She dared to challenge his leadership of the Ophites... impudent child.*

"You now lead the Ophites?" His voice dripped with menace.

El-on-ah's chin tilted, her eyes flashing.

"Indeed, I do, Fyre Meister, and there are thousands of us out there, thousands of Afterlanders who have sworn allegiance to the djinn. As their leader, I can rally them to your cause. We have shared common enemies for many centuries. Since when, millennia ago, the Whytes of Rhodium banished the djinn to Erebus for eternity. Imprisoned you in a land of darkness, but for that light provided by the sulphurous fyres burning deep beneath its barren crust. Lord Ka and we Ophites bought about the obliteration of those same Whytes, and we are responsible for your freedom today. Look within yourself Meister Phlegon and you will know I speak the truth."

Ka leant back in his chair. *Smart girl... Ingenious.*

Without speaking, he placed the sticky peach kernel at the centre of the table in front of him. He could see where she was going with this now, offering him an alliance gives him a reason not to have her killed, but why risk so much to come here? Her mission had been to dispose of the Whyte. Surely, she would not have returned if she had failed.

Ka glanced over to Commander Zelron, who despite appearances to the contrary, was paying a significant amount of attention to their conversation.

"It is true," said Ka, warily. "I am intimately aware of the Ophites devotion to the djinn. That said, you Ophites, ascendants or otherwise, cannot offer anything that we cannot just as easily take from you. Assimilation is an exceptionally efficient method of gaining both knowledge and power, without the impediments associated with alliances and diplomacy." His eyes flicked nervously towards Zelron as he continued, his tone measured and intentionally menacing. "Lady El-on-ah, you are either very brave or very foolish to come here expecting me to offer you anything more than I offered your dear departed leader. So, enlighten me as to why I should not assimilate you, as I did Lord Ka and every other Ophite, who has been unwise enough to cross my path. Elucidate me why don't you?"

He felt his left eye twitch as his gaze fired a warning at El-on-ah's challenging, almond-shaped, black pools. He squirmed in his chair, his impatience growing. He needed to know if she had succeeded. What of his Nemesis, this Rose of the Whyte? Unspoken, the words passed between them.

"I can offer you crucial information regarding a powerful common enemy of ours, together with my skills as an Alchemist to aid your efforts to defeat them." El-on-ah's eyes flicked nervously towards Zelron before meeting Ka's with a look of such piercing intensity that he guessed instantly what she was about to reveal.

"I can confirm," she said, her voice suddenly hushed, "that after more than a thousand years, a Whyte ascendant walks once more in these lands, and I have witnessed a power within her that I have not seen before in one so young. The Sooth has named her Rose, and as prophesied, she seeks Lord Eldwyn's incantatio. She and her cell have already uncovered the first part of the incantation. I trust that you are aware of this spell. It is written that with Eldwyn's incantatio, the Whyte will have the capability to defeat not only we Ophites but you also Meister Phlegon, and your Afreet."

Ka's scowl of fury was genuine. This girl has the nerve to stand here before me taunting me with the Whyte I ordered her to destroy. He lunged forward, his hand tightened around El-on-ah's throat.

Frantically she clawed at his fingers attempting to loosen their grip as she sputtered, gasping for air.

"You saw this Whyte?" He spat out the words, almost forgetting himself as he raged. "You got that close to her, and yet you tell me she is still a threat. You offer me your help in defeating this Whyte and yet when you had the opportunity you failed to take it! Tell me why I should believe that the next time will be any different?"

Releasing his grip on her, he pushed her backwards into the clutches an Afreet guard. They steadied her, as near to collapse she gasped, coughing as air rasped through her swollen airway.

"I... did take it, I cast... a descent spell," she said, "but I my attempt was thwarted. They showed that they are willing to sacrifice their lives for her. Her followers are growing; I believe... she intends to form an allegiance with the Elder Witch and the Twocasts of the Ebony forest."

Ka had no knowledge of the Elder Witch though he knew of the Twocasts, exiled crossbreds who had little power and were certainly no threat to the djinn.

"...and I need you now because?" Ka, snorted. She must have a better plan than this surely.

He could not help her if she did not help herself. Folding his arms, he forced a smile, which was filled with such malevolence that El-on-ah's eyes clouded instantly. She was afraid; maybe this was what he needed to reassure Zelron and his Afreet of his identity. Meister Phlegon would not hesitate to take pleasure in toying with the girl before ultimately destroying her. He had to be prepared to do the same. He was determined to maintain his façade, whatever it took.

"Well?" he said.

There was mischief in his eyes as he watched El-on-ah's uncertainty and alarm rapidly transform into an unbridled panic. He had always enjoyed torturing his subjects; it made them so much more malleable.

"You need me Meister Phlegon," El-on-ah's voice was hoarse, "because though you may have Lord Ka's knowledge, you do not have the ability to channel his potens. If we are to believe the prophecy, then Rose the Whyte can only be defeated through magic. It is the one thing that can counter Eldwyn's incantatio and for that, Meister Phlegon, you need me."

"Maybe..." he said, sardonically, "but then again, maybe not..."

He felt a sudden twinge of pride in his protégé. She had put forward the only argument that would enable him to keep her alive without raising the suspicions of the Djinn. Though Ka still had access to his potens, Phlegon would not have. He could not use his magic without revealing his true identity. Still, magic may not be the only way to deal with Rose the Whyte.

He swung around to face his Afreet Commander.

"Zelron, ready a battalion of Afreet," he shot a look at El-on-ah, his lips twisting into a sadistic leer, "in a battle between fyre and a forest Lady El-on-ah, on which would you place your bet?"

"No!" El-on-ah, struggled against her restraints as Zelron turned to leave. "My servants, Che and Tu-nek-ta are Rose's prisoners, and the Twocasts have young children with them, we don't have to..."

"What a terrible shame my dear," Ka drew his brows together in a mockingly pained expression, "but your servants are almost certainly already dead and the children, well... collateral damage I'm afraid my dear, casualties of war."

"Lock her up until I have decided whether she can be of further use," He glanced up at one of the Afreet officers at her side, "and I'll need her ring. It would not do for her to escape again would it?"

Ka clamped his hand over El-on-ah lips as she attempted to protest. His eyes held her, their communication, subtle - Hold your tongue, or else.

"I think that I have listened to your voice enough for one day my dear," Ka saw his own grotesque features reflected in El-on-ah's beautiful, black, reproachful eyes.

He had felt sure that she had been about to expose him. It was, after all, he who had facilitated her previous escape, but maybe his performance as Phlegon had been a little too good.

The guard pulled on El-on-ah's arm and offered her right hand to Ka. Without taking his eyes from hers, Ka pulled the potens ring from her finger. As he did so, he moved the tip of his forefinger along the centre palm, tracing the outline of the Ouroboros symbol. Her hand had tensed before she attempted to pull it away, but he gripped it tightly, his claw-like fingers digging deep into her flesh. El-on-ah's eyes narrowed accusingly, and then she lifted her head and spat in his face.

His reaction was instinctive. The full force of his fist hitting her square in the face. The power of the blow wrenched her from the Djinn's grip and propelled her body into the wall. A dull thud echoed around the room as her skull smashed into the polished marble. El-on-ah's body teetered for a second with her stunned, accusatory expression still frozen on her face, then her eyes rolled backwards and she crumpled to the floor.

Ka's troubled gaze shifted quickly from El-on-ah's broken body to his fist, clenched tightly and throbbing painfully before him. Puzzled, he turned his wrist, examining his hand, stretching out his fingers, clenching, and then opening them once again. He had not intended to be that brutal. *What is happening to me?*

His bewildered eyes fell on El-on-ah's body, twisted and unmoving at his feet, her red hair soaked and matted with blood. The sickly, metallic odour filled his nostrils.

The horrific realisation hit him like a series of waves, each revelation more powerful and terrifying than the last. He recalled the previous night, their two naked forms writhing in erotic pleasure. His body had betrayed him then, and now, once more it had reacted against his will. *I may have control of my mind, but it is Meister Phlegon who possesses this body and I must find a way to take it back.*

- CHAPTER FIVE -

BELTANE

The village swam with a sea of relaxed faces. The children's smiles emerged from colourfully painted cats, flowers, and foxes, each face brightly decorated with plant-dyed clay. The women and children enjoyed the last of the celebrations as the remnants of the setting sun sparkled through the trees and a ghostly mantle of early evening mist began to creep in along the ground, spilling in from the rapidly darkening forest.

Ferrish fiddle music, softly muffled by the damp air, played merrily in accompaniment to a group of young girls dancing barefoot around the great elder tree. Their hands clasped sprays of brightly coloured rushes as they bobbed and gyrated, eking out one final moment of joyous abandon before the festival ended, as prematurely as it had begun. Old women, distant, wistful expressions resting uncomfortably on their weathered faces, began clearing the remnants of their simple feast. Bread, nuts, dried and honeyed fruits, liquorice root, berry wines and cheeses were whisked from the tables outside each of the dwellings and stowed away, ready for their impending journey. Their sweet aromas lingered in the air like the scent of spun sugar from a summer fayre.

Vega's woman, Lyra, sat on the steps of their wagon with their children, watching the dancing. Lily, her face a mask of painted flowers, and Tau, bearing an uncanny resemblance to a pharmacon loris, rested their heads on their mother and fought to keep their heavy-lidded eyes open. Vega watched them from inside the wagon as he stowed the last of the supplies, his poignant, pensive smile fading as he looked out over the edge of the clearing. Two figures, seemingly oblivious to the festivities, looked away, their eyes cast up towards the southern sky.

Rose and Ash paced nervously along the edge of the clearing meticulously examining the skyline. Rose, feeling Vega's eyes upon her, turned and glanced back. She saw Vega's faint smile vanish as he caught sight of her expression. *He reads me as effortlessly as he does the leaves in a cup.* Feeling uncomfortably vulnerable, she turned back towards Ash.

"We need to go," she folded her arms in frustration, "why is it taking them so long… This dallying is madness!"

"Relax Rose," Ash's relaxed smile belied the unease in his eyes. "This may be the last time they get to let their hair down for a while, and a few more minutes are unlikely to make much difference. Going ahead with the festival was a good idea, just look over there."

He jerked his head towards a group of children happily chuckling as they joined the dancers, skipping around the tree; their stubby feet, bare and blackened by the dusty ground.

Rose smiled despite her anxiety, but the smile was fleeting, vanishing as her eyes fell on a small Twocast girl. The girl's mass of red hair bounced on her shoulders as she skipped merrily around the tree with the others. Instantly, Rose recalled the scene that they had witnessed in the Sooth only days before. The image of that red-haired child, burning to death in the fyre of the Afreet had been seared into her mind forever. It returned to her again and again, stealing each brief moment of joy and haunting her dreams. Rose blinked, swallowing hard, as she felt the briny heat pool in her eyes.

"Rose?" Ash's eyes narrowed in concern.

The last thing Rose wanted was for Ash to be kind to her. That would be too much. *I have cried enough.*

She looked past him, her face stoically expressionless as she watched two figures approaching from the centre of the village. She stepped out, striding doggedly towards them as she called back over her shoulder.

"I'm fine, but it's time we left, I have no intention of watching any more children burn."

Ash fell in behind her, he made no comment, seeming to sense her mood.

Ro-eh-na and Commander Linden were engaged in a heated argument. Linden, newly equipped with a Twocast bow and quiver full of arrows, wore a face like thunder. By the time Rose and Ash reached the pair of them their angry exchanges had ceased, though their clenched jaws and scowling eyes told the same story.

"Do we have a problem?" Rose lifted her brows, looking to each of them in turn for an answer.

An awkward silence followed, then both attempted to speak at once. The anger and frustration in their words being the only thing that Rose could discern from the resulting din.

"Hold on," Rose was irritated. Why are they arguing when all of our lives are in imminent danger? "I did not get a word of that. Ro-eh-na, you speak." Rose held up a hand as Linden tried to interject. "You'll have your say in a moment... Ro-eh-na?"

"He says that I cannot go with you," said Ro-eh-na, her voice quick and tight. "He says that I will slow you down, that I'll be a liability and that I should go with Elder to Isingwilde."

"Well, look at her... she can hardly walk," Linden's exasperation was evident. "If we are to make good time to Ogin's Deep, then she will have to travel in the wagon with the children and the wagon is not accompanying us to Kelpievale, so how can she possibly come with us?"

Rose glanced from Linden's glowering face to Ro-eh-na's fractured expression of exasperation and then to Ash. His look of barely disguised amusement infected her immediately causing her to chuckle and then to laugh. Soon the three of them were laughing uncontrollably. Lindens frustration turned to bewilderment.

"Ro-eh-na, did you not explain..." Rose giggled, desperately attempting to regain her composure.

"Actions speak louder than words," said Ash with a wink in Ro-eh-na's direction.

Ro-eh-na nonchalantly shrugged her shoulders. Then her mouth lifted in a wry, slanted smile as she mumbled an incantation.

"Transmutes niue pardus."

Her potens ring flashed. Its pulsating light expanded around her, enveloping her in a luminous mist. The glistening haze transformed into the shape of a large white leopard, bounding forward, its incandescent glow trailing behind, like the tail of a comet, before vanishing to reveal the full magnificence of the great animal. Thick, sleek white fur covered its body and framed two piercing black eyes, peering out from the face of the Rhodium snow leopard.

Slowly, the creature circled the three of them before turning its attention to Linden. Fangs bared, a low ominous growl escaped its gaping jaws. Linden's eyes widened, his hand reached automatically for the hilt of his sword. Then, cursing to himself, he re-sheathed it, lifting his palms in mock surrender as he stepped backwards away from the approaching feline.

"Okay… okay…," said Ash with a grin "Ro-eh-na, you've made your point, no need to underline it with blood."

"And, enjoyable as this is," said Rose, "we do need to get going."

"I came to tell you that everything is ready," Linden regarded the pacing leopard warily as he spoke to Rose. "Essential belongings and food have been packed, and the wagon is loaded. All that remains is to get the children on board before we leave."

The fiddle music finally ceased and the air quietened, but for a muted chorus of disappointed cries from a few weary children.

"Great," Rose gave a small sigh of relief. The delay, with the sense of urgency that she was feeling had generated a growing knot of anxiety inside her. She felt as if she had been holding her breath for days. "Let's go then. We need to reach the cover of the Winter Forest before daybreak, and that's not going to be easy with so many of them not even owning a pair of shoes."

Rose remembered her feelings of pity when they had first entered the village. The villagers followed Vega's wagon, their feet were mostly bare or wrapped in rabbit skins tied on with hemp twine. She had felt ashamed then, she had wanted to make things right. *Is that what I am doing, making things right? How can they be expected to survive in the north without even the most basic equipment? I could be sending them to their deaths, but if they stay here...*

The clatter of hoofs and the gentle rumble of cartwheels pulled her out of her reverie. Vega's wagon approached, straining under the weight of its cargo, the children, the old and the infirm. Vastly overladen, it rocked, lurching dangerously on the uneven ground.

Behind the wagon, a line of Twocasts walked three or four abreast. Each of them carried all their worldly possessions, stuffed into sacks and tied to their backs with leather straps or hemp twine that cut deep into their shoulders as they walked. They appeared to have dressed as well as they could for the icy weather ahead of them, their feet wrapped in roughly sewn rabbit skin boots and their bodies cloaked in bizarre, shapeless fur cloaks, fashioned from a diverse collection of animal skins.

Behind them came the High Councillors and the other Muds from Glynisfarne. Officer Blackthorn accompanied El-on-ah's two spies, Che & Tu-nek-ta. Under the effects of *Oblitus* potion, their cheery, gormless smiles were in bizarre contrast to their vacant, glassy stares.

Auriel, Lee, and the Elder Witch followed at the rear of the convoy. Elder wore a thick, grey woollen cloak. Rose noticed the increasing frequently with which she was using her staff to steady her tall, gaunt frame as she walked. Her feet were bare.

As the cart rattled towards them, Vega lifted his weatherworn hat in greeting, snapping the reins and driving the horses on. He chuckled as Rose and Ash jumped backwards, the wheels having pitched violently sideways, almost mowing them down.

"Aye," he said, twisting around as he passed, "you'd be wise t' remember rule number twenty-seven... never get in the way of a fully laden cart."

Rose shook her head, sharing a smile of exasperation with Ash.

"I'm not sure which is the scariest," Ash's lips twitched, "the Afreet with their fyre spears, or Vega with his wagon."

After the bedraggled procession had passed, Rose's group fell into line at the back. Auriel handed her a small sack packed with provisions, Lee tossed a similar one to Ash.

Auriel's eyes widened as she glanced towards the snow leopard padding softly at Rose's side.

"Ro-eh-na," said Rose, "she could come in quite useful in that form, don't you think?"

Sloley, seemingly unimpressed by the addition of the large white cat to their group, let out series of frantic shrieks and screeches before diving into the hood of Lee's cloak and burying himself deep inside the soft material.

Rose felt her anxiety ease a little as they made their way out of the forest. Now that they were on their way, she felt oddly content with her friends walking purposefully at her side.

Ahead of them, Vega's cart bobbed along rhythmically, trailed by its ragtag procession of individuals.

The evening mist billowed in around their feet, swirling above the wagon's wheels until it appeared to float like a tiny vessel, adrift on a vast, alabaster sea.

To Rose, the chilly, moist night air smelled fresh, like a new beginning. Tonight they were leaving behind the dark, musty dwellings, the choking wood smoke, and the putrid stench of the stink holes. She smiled; at least, no one will ever have to visit them again.

As they finally left the cover of the forest, soft echoes of children's voices drifted up on the night breeze.

'Hush little bairn, keep thee silent,
It's nay the time for your lament,
Thy Ma she's tired and thy Pa he's worn,
So keep thee a sleepin' 'til the morn...'

Soon, the only sounds in the night air were the hollow clatter of the wagon's wheels, the faint sporadic hum of muffled voices and the gentle padding of tired, wet feet over the cold, damp ground. The night sky, growing blacker with every second, showed little sign of what was to come.

- CHAPTER SIX -

OGIN'S DEEP

Rose, Ash and Elder were the last of the group to reach the summit of the hill, known to the Ferrish as 'Flat Top.' The peak rose from the flatlands as if some immense giant had upturned their empty cup, setting it down by the side of Ogin's Deep until nature had claimed it, cloaking it with earth and moss. The vast expanse of brackish water, known as Ogin's Deep, had long been the focus of much Ferrish superstition. The Mud's believed it to be a place of great evil, the realm of water wraiths, knuckers and Fae, all of them intent on dragging unsuspecting mortals deep into its bottomless depths.

Vega's wagon and the majority of the Twocasts were well ahead and had begun making their way down into the valley. They had been travelling all night. Initially, Rose thought that Elder was coping well with the journey, considering her age, but now that they were within a few miles of their destination, it was becoming apparent that the old woman was beginning to struggle.

"Here," she said, offering her hand.

Elder hesitated, staring at Rose's outstretched hand as if it were a poisoned chalice.

"Elder please, there is no shame in borrowing strength from younger limbs. We need to move faster, and we will not leave you behind."

Relenting with a sigh, Elder took her hand. Rose cast a glance towards Ash, who instantly caught her meaning and lent his support. With their help, Elder took the last few steps to the summit.

Linden, Auriel, Lee, and Ro-eh-na were waiting, a few feet ahead of them. Ro-eh-na, still in the form of a large white leopard, had doggedly stayed within a few feet of Rose during the entire journey. A silent, white shadow, the big cat tracked Rose's every move and it had begun to irk her somewhat.

Surveying the summit, Rose could see how the hill had got its name. The top truly was flat and this allowed them to see for miles in every direction. Stretched out to the North was the vast expanse of dark water known as Ogin's Deep. The moonlight glinted off its black surface, scattering shards of light over towards its northeast edge and silhouetting the snow-tipped trees, marking the southeastern boundary of the Winter Forest. The North wind whipped through the air, scalding her cheeks and driving specks of frozen rain into her skin like icy needles.

"We should just make it before dawn," she said, almost to herself, "are you alright to go on now Elder, or do you need to rest a while?"

She glanced down at the old woman's feet; bare, cut, bruised, and blue with cold.

"You need not trouble yourself with me," Elder spoke sharply. Then, shaking her head wearily, she softened her tone. "No, thank you, Rose. We need to get everyone beneath the cover of the trees before sunrise. I'll rest when my people are safe."

"I fear that time has passed, Dawn is breaking as we speak." Linden's gaze rested above their heads and out towards the distant horizon.

The sky glowed golden, awash with light and shimmering hues of crimson and orange.

Elder swung around, teetering momentarily, as she steadied herself, hands tightly gripping her staff.

"That is no sunrise," her voice was small and tight.

Elder had spoken the words so quietly that Rose could barely distinguish them from the wind whistling eerily around them.

"Unless our sun decided it needed a change and so would rise in the south this day," Something flickered behind Elder's limpid violet eyes.

Rose recognised that look. It was the expression that had lit her own eyes when El-on-ah had taken Arjan from her. It was grief. Rose followed Elder's doleful gaze, squinting towards the horizon. Immediately she grasped the reason behind Elder's melancholia.

"It's the Afreet, isn't it?" she said, "They're burning the Ebony Forest, they must believe we are still there."

"Aye, it seems that we owe you another debt, my dear. If you had not been so insistent that we left immediately..." Her voice trailed off as she stole a pensive glance towards the glowing horizon. "Let us hope that they do not search the ashes too vigilantly."

Rose bit down hard on her lip as she regarded the flaming southern skyline. What must it be like to live a thousand years in one place? To grow to love and lead the people, to witness the birth and death of generation after generation. How can anyone cope with that volume of loss, over and over again, and now, to lose the only home you have ever known and yet still have hope... These people have an incredible leader and it's not me.

"They would be foolish not to investigate thoroughly," Rose placed her hand over Elders bony fingers, squeezing them gently, "and I don't believe Lord Ka is stupid. He will expect them to bring back proof of our demise. So we have only hours before they discover that we escaped their attack. We need to move more quickly now if we are to keep your people safe."

The large white leopard padded silently over towards her, burying its muzzle in Rose's palm. Glancing down into Ro-eh-na's large feline eyes Rose heard the Blood's thoughts as clearly as if she had spoken them. It always unnerved her how some metamorphs were able to communicate so effortlessly through thought.

"Elder," Rose's eyes flicked up to meet the old woman's, "Ro-eh-na, asks that you would grant her the honour of carrying you to the Winter Forest."

Elder's jaw momentarily tightened, but her brief expression of stubborn willfulness was quickly replaced with one of stoic acceptance.

"Aye," she said with a sigh, "so long as Ro-eh-na accepts that we will remain at the rear of the convoy. I will have none of my people come after me. They should see that I do not value myself over them."

"My dear Elder," Rose was rapidly warming to this prickly old woman. "If they have not yet learned that, then they never will. Come, we must be on our way."

Without notice, and ignoring her protests Commander Linden lifted Elder effortlessly into his arms and placed her gently on the leopard's back.

The seven of them made their way rapidly down the hillside towards Vega's Wagon. Ahead of them, the procession of Twocasts was fast disappearing behind a curtain of heavy snow and frozen rain, as they trudged along the dirt road towards Winter Forest.

They reached the edge of the Forest a few hours later, just as dawn was breaking and the blizzard had begun to ease. Towards the east, the distant Ice Mountains changed with every passing minute. Magnificent, glistening shards of morning sunlight rose from behind them, like a flaming crown, each fiery ray splashing garlands of crimson and gold along the jagged horizon. Under its dazzling light, even Ogin's Deep appeared welcoming, it's cold blackness warmed by glimmers of amber, gleaming like flecks of quartz in polished black marble.

The road into the forest once blanketed in freshly fallen snow, now lay strewn with the evidence of their passing. The heavily laden cart and hundreds of tired feet had left a trail that could have been followed by a blind man. As the last of the procession disappeared under the cover of the trees, Rose stood at the edge of the thicket and gazed back at the muddy trail, which extended out from Flat Top like a giant black finger signposting their location.

"Hmm," said Ash, cupping his chin in his hand, "don't you think maybe that's a little too subtle... There is a tiny chance that the Afreet could miss it. Why don't we just erect a giant sign that says Rose and the resistance this way?"

A loud screech from above startled them all; their eyes darted upwards. In unison, they followed the swooping flight of a snow owl as it barked its alarm call out into the frosty morning air.

"We could," said Elder smiling, "but I may have a somewhat more acceptable solution..."

Raising her staff in the air, she pointed the green crystal hilt out towards the road.

"nix ictu iter tegere," She cast the incantation with the easy self-assurance of a Magister.

Rose watched as the large uncut crystal glowed, pulsating briefly before emitting a thin stream of emerald light that snaked out towards the road, zigzagging across the fields on either side of the trail, darting over their tracks and whipping the snow up into the air. It hung there fleetingly for a second, like a moth-eaten curtain, before falling onto the road and blanketing it with a thick layer of white.

She may not be an Ascendant in the real sense of the word, thought Rose, but she cast that spell like an expert.

Ash grinned at Lee whose mouth gaped open like a hungry hatchling. Raising an eyebrow, Lee turned a questioning eye towards Elder.

"It's not just ascendants who can learn to control the elements," She smiled wryly.

Yes, but who had been there to teach her? The more Rose discovered about Elder, the more of a mystery the woman became.

They made camp on the north-west side of the forest where the brittle, frosted trees spread out in a line that followed the slope of the land, descending almost to the edge of Ogin's Deep. With their gnarled branches silhouetted against the morning sunlight, they looked like a line of old men who, in preparing to take a dip in the icy black water, had been twisted and frozen in their tracks by a sudden ice storm.

The morning sun warmed the frosted branches causing the frozen snow to melt and steam, spawning a hazy fog that wafted up in delicate wisps, shimmering in the sunlight like spun silver. The children who had slept, blissfully unaware of the trials of the journey, were now awake, and their giggles and easy laughter filled the air, mingling with the rhythmic sound of the men chopping wood and the clatter of the women folk unpacking equipment and preparing breakfast.

Rose was aware of this hive of activity though she listened with an air of detachment. Having slipped away from the campsite, she sat silently on the trunk of a fallen tree and looked out over Ogin's Deep.

Rose desperately needed to sleep and yet her mind would not settle and soon filled with anxious thoughts of Ka and the Djinn, and of the battle ahead. Her feet ached so much that the urge to plunge them into the freezing water, just to numb their pain, was almost irresistible. As if sensing her thoughts, a sea hawk's cry pierced the air as it plunged like an arrow into the water, barely making a splash. A series of ripples spread out across the otherwise flat expanse of water. *Every act has its ripples.* She recalled Arjan's fatal expression as he left her, a final portrait of all of his pain, anguish, and sorrow. *Yet no regret. Why no regret?* It had always puzzled her.

The hawk emerged from the waters depths, its enormous wings straining to drag its sodden, feathered body into the air, a giant writhing silver fish clasped in its talons. The struggle was a short one. Once clear of the pull of the water the bird soared effortlessly into the sky. It flew out towards the eastern mountains, it's wings tipped with golden light. Rose tracked the path of its flight, lifting her hand to shade her eyes from the glare of the sun, now sitting high on the summit of the mountain like a giant golden egg, balanced precariously on the edge of its cliff top nest.

"It's beautiful isn't it?" Ash wrenched his eyes from her melancholy face and followed her gaze.

Rose hadn't heard him approach. She felt briefly irritated by his intrusion, but she could not stay angry at Ash for long, few people could, not even Lee.

"I had hoped for a little time alone," Her tone barely hinted at her exasperation. "Ro-eh-na has not left my side for a second since we left. I needed some time to think."

"Why yes Ash, you are right, the sunrise is truly breath-taking…" Ash waved a hand towards the glowing horizon before moving it over his heart and continuing breathlessly. "I am so glad that you are here with me to share this moment; you are indeed a truly exceptional…"

Rose could not avert the smile that sprung to her lips as she turned to look at him. Ash's expression was pretty much as she expected. His lopsided grin and gently mocking green eyes glinted with mischief and warmth. He could always be relied on to cheer her up no matter how bad things got.

"I'm sorry," she said, feeling ashamed. Why do I always take everything out on him?

Her eyes stung as she looked back at the panoramic view of the Ice Mountains, glowing golden in the sunlight.

"You're right Ash, it is beautiful, breathtaking in fact, but we can't stay here, we need to leave. Every moment we spend with these people puts them at risk. They'll be safer without us. I don't want to be responsible for any more deaths."

Unconsciously she fingered Arjan's apis pin.

Ash frowned, his green eyes narrowing as his smile dissolved. Rose saw the compassion and uncertainty on his face, and she knew what he was going to say even before he spoke the words. It was a lie she had told herself over and over again.

"Rose, you are not responsible for any deaths," tentatively, he reached out and took her arm. "Arjan chose his fate, it was a noble and brave choice, and you should not take that away from him. What Elder said earlier is right. If you had not pushed us, we would all have died today. Today you have saved lives Rose, hundreds of lives. If you have to dwell on anything, dwell on that."

"Fine, maybe you and Elder are right," she groaned, unable to shake the image of Arjan from her mind. "But that does not alter the fact that every second we spend here we endanger those very same lives. I don't think that we can afford to wait, even for nightfall. We should go now. I've been thinking, and I have a plan. We can travel by daylight if we follow the edge of Ogin's Deep it's in a natural basin, and that will provide cover for us, see…"

She traced her outstretched finger in the air following along the ridge overhanging the shoreline.

Feeling the excitement build inside her, Rose's words came quickly as the germs of an idea solidified into a cohesive plan in her mind.

"See how the salt water, pebbles, and sand have caused the snow to melt along the shoreline," she continued eagerly, "it means that we won't even have to worry about leaving tracks."

"Rose, it's not that I don't see the sense in what you are saying," Ash looked away from her instantly reproachful eyes. Then, after a moment's hesitation he turned to confront her, determinately taking her face into his hands, forcing her to look at him, their noses almost touching, "but look at you, Rose, you are exhausted. We are all exhausted. At the very least you need to allow everyone time to eat and sleep before asking more of them because if you ask more of them, Rose, then they will readily respond and I honestly believe that would be a mistake. If we are to attempt to cross Ogin's Deep into Rhodium, then we need to be rested. It is not an easy route."

Rose tried to make a serious consideration his words, but her mind was in a whirl. Ash had moved so close that she could feel his breath on her skin and all she seemed able to focus on was the colour of his eyes. She had never noticed before how green they were, a thick carpet of emerald moss littered with golden leaves.

"Rose, are you listening to me?" Ash's tilted, mocking smile returned, "Rose, your eyes are open but are you by any chance... sleeping?"

"No, no I was just thinking..." Rose blinked out of her reverie, "that you're right. Obviously, I must be pretty exhausted, I can't even think straight."

"Then allow me to escort you back,"

She sensed Ash's relief as he leant back and offered her his bended elbow. Hesitantly she took his arm.

"Lee and Auriel are cooking up a fyre-pot," he said, grinning, "and when you've eaten and rested your thoughts will be much clearer, you'll see. A few hours rest won't hurt Rose."

Maybe, she thought, feeling a pang of hunger as she caught the delicious aroma of hot food as they approached the campsite.

"Eggs and bacon?" Ash said as Rose pronounced, "Waffles!"

Then together, "Fyre-pot!"

"Hey, you two," Auriel ran to greet them. "Lee and I made a Fyre-pot, and none of the Twocasts have ever tasted anything like it before…. They're going crazy!"

Rose wondered what the fyre-pot must taste like to them. The dish is enchanted so that it tastes of whatever you crave the most. The Twocasts had tasted few delicacies, how could they imagine the taste of ice cream, or chocolate, or venison in red wine. Though if they had ever tasted something delicious, then it is not surprising that they were acting as if it were Beltane all over again.

As Rose reached the campsite, the carnival atmosphere cheered her immediately. The Twocasts gathered around a large campfire at the centre of the clearing. There was the usual cacophony of sound she had come to expect from Twocast gatherings. Two young men sat on logs strumming their lutes and singing while others played jigs on their fiddles as the children danced. Most sat cross-legged on blankets and fleeces laid out on the frozen ground, their hands cupped around large bowls of fyre-pot stew. The steaming, pink mixture deposited a mist of tiny droplets on their faces giving them a rosy, dewy glow. Rose smiled at the ecstasy in their expressions. This is how magic should be used, not to harm, not to kill.

Lee stood behind an enormous copper cauldron, which bubbled over a small, smouldering fire at the front of Vega's wagon. He waved large ladle at them as they approached and then spooned the remains of the stew into two small bowls.

"Where have you been?" Lee shook his head with a theatrical sigh. "Everyone is waiting for you inside. Here, you had better take these with you. I cannot believe that you picked this time to disappear."

Ash grinned mischievously. He took the bowls from Lee and handed one to Rose with a conspiratorial wink.

"Oh... you know how it is, we had important things to discuss," he said. "Some of us are born to assist in the planning next of the next, vital and very dangerous mission, whereas others it seems, are more suited, to... cooking stew."

Lee's expression gave little away, his emotions, as always, kept tightly under his control. Sloley, on the other hand, was much more vocal. Perched, as was usual on Lee's shoulder, the loris let out a series of clicks and squeaks, epitomising exactly how irritated Lee must have felt.

If ever I need insight into Lee's feelings, thought Rose, all I have to do is watch Sloley.

"You do realise," Lee brows arched, though the movement was so slight, it was barely distinguishable, "If I were to add just one further ingredient to your bowl, I could render you completely silent for the next month at least. The more you talk, the more appealing that seems. So, keep it up why don't you."

"You do realise," Ash, smirked good-humouredly, "that if ever you did manage to render me speechless, then I'd transform into a tiny apis and buzz so loudly inside your ear that you'd be begging for mercy within minutes. So knock yourself out why don't you…"

"Ye have nay time for socialising," Vega's head emerged from behind the wagon's canopy.

"We've been waiting for ya for a while now and some in 'ere are growing impatient."

"We'll be right there," said Rose, shaking her head and glancing from Ash to Lee. They were incorrigible. Listening to them anyone would think that they hated each other. How can a great wizard like Eldwyn put so much trust in the four of us, when in so many ways we are still children?

The wagon was more crowded than Rose had expected. Although it now held a similar number of people as earlier, when they travelled into the Ebony forest, previously, it had not contained Commander Linden. His large frame barely squeezed into a seat made for two. Elder and Lord Alder stood at the back while everyone else remained seated. Tarik, Marshal Shadbush, Hazel and Lord Elm sat on the right and to the left sat Commander Linden and Ro-eh-na,

"Ah, good you are here," said Elder "take a seat and we will get started. Alder and I have been discussing our plans, in the light of the Afreet's recent attack on the Ebony Forest."

Rose sat down next to Ro-eh-na, the others somehow, managing to squash in next to Commander Linden. Ash lowered himself into his seat. Hesitating, he looked longingly at the bowl of steaming stew in his hand. After glancing around, he lifted the bowl to his mouth and took a hasty gulp of the thick, pink coloured concoction.

Rose pressed her lips together stifling a smile as she watched the look of rapture spread across his face, now embellished by a bright pink ring about his mouth. The pink lipstick should have made him look ridiculous, but instead, it only seemed to emphasise the masculinity of his features and his sharply chiselled jaw line. Rose placed her bowl on the floor under her seat.

"Alder and I think that it would be better if your group left sooner rather than later," Elder got straight to the point. "Once the Afreet realise that we have left the forest they will come after us. We cannot risk them discovering you, and you will all travel much faster unencumbered by a large group, especially when it contains so many who are old and infirm, and so many children. A large group such as ours will be much easier to spot from the air, whereas the six of you on foot should be better able to avoid detection."

"I agree," Rose said, relieved that she did not need to convince them of her plan to depart sooner. "You should travel only at night until you are well into Rhodium. I doubt that they will look for us this far north, but it would be prudent to lay low during daylight hours and stay hidden beneath the tree canopy. We, on the other hand, must get going as soon as we can. I have a way to keep us out of sight while we travel."

She hesitated as she grasped the unspoken question that flickered in Linden's eyes.

"We can use the lip of the basin around Ogin's Deep for cover. It has quite a wide overhang, which should make it possible for us to journey by day," Rose hesitated, feeling suddenly uncomfortable. *Maybe I should have consulted him before presenting it to everyone else?* "What do you think Commander?"

"The plan has merit," Linden nodded thoughtfully, seemingly content with her albeit belated, recognition of his expert military opinion. "However, if they do decide to search to the North, then travelling by daylight will make us very vulnerable. Though I agree it is unlikely the Afreet will look towards Rhodium initially, so the quicker we leave Ferrum, the less chance of them discovering us."

"My reasoning exactly," Rose twisted her potens ring around on her finger.

She had expected protests to come flooding from this sea of exhausted faces, but there were none. Rose looked at each of their tired, gaunt faces and realised that Ash had been right, and so she made another unilateral decision.

"However, Ash has convinced me that we could all benefit from a couple of hours sleep, so I suggest that we leave around noon. With this short delay, we should still aim to arrive at the Kelpidale landing before dawn tomorrow. It will be safer to cross Ogin's Deep before the sun is up. Does anyone object to any of this?"

Ash gulped down the last of his stew and bought his sleeve across his face in an unsuccessful attempt to remove the pink stain from his lips. Clearing his throat, he tentatively raised his hand. Rose sensed his nervousness.

Ash was always willing to act the fool, it was part of his charm, but few people took him seriously because of it. Rose knew him better than that; Ash used his wit like armour. If no one takes you seriously, then no one judges you. Acting the fool is one thing, being judged a fool is another.

"I don't have an objection," Ash hesitated, "I have a suggestion."

"Go on," Elder gestured for him to continue.

"I think I could save us time if I travelled ahead, on the wing," said Ash. "I can be in Kelpiedale within a few hours. Then I'd have plenty of time to arrange for some transport across the Ogin's Deep and gather supplies. With fewer supplies to carry you would be able to travel much lighter, and faster. I can meet you at the landings with everything sorted so we'll be able to cross as soon as you arrive. I know there would be one less to protect Rose on the journey to Kelpidale but…"

"No, that's fine," said Rose, "It's an excellent idea Ash, and truthfully, I think I have enough protection."

"Well, that's fine for you then," Hazel's mouth twisted. "You make quite sure that you're well protected won't you, with a Mage, an Alchemist, two Metamorphs, a Memorix and the Commander of the Lignum Vitae? Who is going to be looking out for the rest of us? A handful of Memorix, a Civil Councillor, a second-rate soldier and a worthless collection of Twocasts. Hardly a match for the Afreet army are we?"

The noise of the campsite, the clanking of pots, music and laughter faded away as her words pierced the air like a poisoned dart. The silence expanded, engulfing them like a vacuum, every sound compressed into one tiny spark, which threatened to explode at any second. Then, just as the faintest distant rumble precedes the fiercest storm, Elder's words, when they came, seemed innocuous.

"You omitted to include me in your appraisal," she said deliberately, "exactly where do I figure in your little hierarchy?"

Rose could sense the tension, but as she watched Lee's eyes widen as he glanced nervously between the two women, she struggled to suppress a smile of amusement. Hazel not only appeared to be the only person unaware of the thinness of the ice on which she stood, but she also seemed quite oblivious to the consequences of recklessly skating out into the middle of it.

"It's not my hierarchy," Hazel lifted her chin boldly, "it is an accepted chain of command long set down by our ancestors, one that has been in existence for thousands of years and one which I am certain will reinstate when normality is restored to our world."

Elder leant on her staff, bringing her fragile, wizened face to within inches of Hazel's perfectly smooth, symmetrical features.

"The world of which you speak no longer exists," Elder murmured, "there is no longer room for hierarchies or their redundant figureheads. You need to adjust to a new reality, Lady Hazel. Nature teaches us the consequences that befall all those who fail to adapt."

The two women scowled at each other like circling cats.

"Yes, well, I for one am in no doubt that Rose's plan is sound," Alder cleared his throat in an attempt to disrupt the tension. Neither woman flinched. "Look, we are all of us tired and tempers are frayed. We all need some rest. As Rose suggested, she and her group can take a couple of hours sleep before leaving around noon. The rest of us will remain here until just before dusk. Then we head northeast under cover of the tree canopy. We'll circle Ogin's Deep and trek into Rhodium via the foothills of the Ice Mountains. Unless," he went on, looking pointedly at Hazel, "anyone has any legitimate objections to this?" He continued immediately not allowing anyone the opportunity to answer. "Good, because none of us will survive if we do not work together, no matter whom we may be."

Rose had watched the storm clouds gather and the winds abate. Like many great twisters, it had left almost everyone untouched. However, Rose had little doubt that Hazel, at least, had caught a glimpse of its potentially devastating power.

Fascinated, Rose could not take her eyes from Hazel as she watched Elder leave the wagon. That perfect porcelain mask revealed little, but for the subtle twitching of one steely green eye and a tight ripple, that ran along the jaw line as perfect white teeth bit hard on her tongue.

- CHAPTER SEVEN -

SINS OF WAR

The door crashed open against the stone wall of El-on-ah's cell. Ka entered the chamber like a thunderbolt.

"Stay there," He screamed at the Afreet guard who had been about to follow him in. "If I wish your presence, I will order it!"

Grabbing the edge of the heavy wooden door he slammed it shut, the officer jumped backwards, barely managing to avoid being hit in the face. Ka's chest heaved, his eyes filling with a mien of fury so intense that El-on-ah realised that her luck had finally run out, he would destroy her now for sure.

"They were gone. All of them," he spat, "not one body in that forest, not even the servants that you abandoned. The Whyte remains a threat to us all because you did not do your job!"

El-on-ah leapt up from her seat on the crude wooden bed. It was the only thing in her cell, but for a threadbare blanket and a slop bucket.

She grasped tightly to the sleeves of her robe, it prevented her hands from shaking as she fought to control her fear. Who is this reptilian monstrosity standing before her, seething with untethered emotion?

She had known Ka to be a ruthless leader, he had struck her more than once, but this display of unbridled emotion was so alien to a Blood. It terrified her, and yet, he was not the only Blood to be gripped by emotion.

El-on-ah had a right to be scared, it would be unnatural not to be afraid of what this monster could be capable of, but her fear was dwarfed by another emotion. A spark of hope kindled within and, like hot soup on a cold day, its gentle heat growing, warming her ashen features. *Che is alive.* The thought restored her soul, renewing its strength and forging her fear into fury.

"I have risked my life to do your bidding!" she hissed. "Risked the life of my servants. I have pledged my allegiance to you my Lord and my loyalty is sound. Why else would I come here? How can you treat me with such disrespect?"

Ka appeared surprised by her sudden reproach. He hesitated for a second, his anger seeming to subside. Maybe he too battles to control his emotions, she thought, or maybe he is just deciding how best to dispose of me.

"You craft a valid argument, my dear," Ka's tone became more subdued. "Maybe I do underappreciate your efforts, but our success lives and dies with the fate of Rose the Whyte. If she survives, then all that we have worked for is lost."

"It is for that very reason that I am here," said El-on-ah. "I came back knowing that I would have to face your wrath. I returned because I believed our cause is worth fighting for, but now I am here…" Pointedly she allowed her eyes to roam around her pitiful cell, "Well frankly, I wonder if any of it was worth it. All your noble intentions seem to be forgotten now my Lord, or am I mistaken?"

"Not forgotten, never forgotten," Ka appeared pensive, his words hesitant, "I promised to give you and the rest of our brethren the world that we craved, a world free from prejudice and discrimination, and I intend to keep my promise. We are fighting for what is rightfully ours, fighting to ensure that Blood children will no longer die in the bowels of the Treymaneor mines nor will their parents perish from the effects of working an entire lifetime below ground. I have never forgotten what we fight for though the means to our success is so much more complicated than I had foreseen. We will realise our dreams El-on-ah, but first, we must win."

El-on-ah recognised many of these words, they came from *The Unification* Lord Ka's autobiographical manifesto, the seminal book in which he outlined his ideology and vision for the future of the Afterlands. The book on which the Ophites movement was built.

Written before the Great Dragon War the book was structured around his central thesis, *'The Whyte Plague'* in which he voiced the existence of a Whyte conspiracy intent on gaining total control of the Afterlands. Ka accused the Councils of Aurum and Ferrum of complacency, he announced his intention to win power and dismantle the system, a system he and many others believed to be corrupt. The book was immediately banned by all of the high councils of the Afterlands, even in Hydrargyrum's Chambers. They called it incendiary and provocative, and they were right.

The book was a catalyst. It rapidly went underground where its popularity grew, primarily amongst the Bloods. Copies of the book were prized, hidden and smuggled throughout the Afterlands. Ka gained a fanatical following, giving birth to the Ophite movement amongst whom he became known as the Great Lord Ka.

Sometime later El-on-ah had begun her service under the great Lord Ka. Ascension after ascension, descent after descent, she had served Lord Ka and his cause for many lifetimes, never questioning, never wavering in her loyalty. Regarding him know, she realised that for the first time, her loyalty was in question, she knew it, and so did he.

Ka did not seem so 'great' to her now, he no longer looked or even acted like a Blood, and until uttering those last few words, he had not sounded like one either. Could she be making a terrible, unforgivable, catastrophic mistake?

"How do you intend to win anything," she said, her voice quivering, "when your support is dwindling, when you are assimilating and imprisoning Ophites as we speak?"

Ka's jaw tightened, his lipless mouth forming into a grotesque scowl.

"I should not need to remind you," He snapped, "that it was your incompetence that resulted in the release of the Djinn. I had little choice but to respond in the way that I did. If I had not, then we would all have been assimilated, or ended up as slaves cowering at the feet of Fyre Meister Phlegon. I took the only option open to me. Reversing the assimilation process has enabled us to take control of the ruling Djinn without the Afreet becoming over suspicious. The assimilations have been generally successful, but for the evident aesthetic insufficiencies."

As he talked, Ka methodically clenched and unclenched his fists.

"Are you sure those are the only inadequacies?"

"Certain," his eyes met hers with a penetrating glare. "I admit that my plans were somewhat hindered by the appearance of the Djinn. However, this may yet work in our favour. We now have an army with the capacity to reach anywhere in the Afterlands within hours."

"But what good is an army against Whyte magic?" She blurted, "More than anyone, you should know that only powerful magic can defeat a Whyte."

"Indeed," Ka's mouth twisted into an ugly grin, "and that is why I am sending you to Rhodium. I want you to collect the minerals required to create fractionation venom."

El-on-ah gasped, surely he can't intend to...

"You intend to use a confractio charm?"

"Well, I think you will agree that last time, I was rather successful in ridding our world of the Whyte plague," he clenched his fist once more. "Indeed, if it hadn't had been for the meddling of Lord Eldwyn, we would not be in this position now. This time, we will not be facing the likes of Lord Eldwyn, just one female novice who has not yet completed her first year at the oratory. Disposing of her should hold as much challenge to us, as swatting a fly, should it not?"

El-on-ah's mind raced, how could he even consider using the confractio again?

When Ka had first used the spell, he could not have known the vast devastation that it would bring, but now everyone knew. The confractio charm had the capacity to inflict death and destruction totally indiscriminately and on a colossal scale. How could he, how could anyone, boast about the obliteration of an entire race? She could not allow him to do it again, could she?

He towered over her; his eyes examined every nuance of her expression. Could he sense her doubt, her disgust? A pang of fear shot through her body. If she refused to obey his orders, he would have her assimilated. El-on-ah feared that more than anything else; descent was one thing, eternal imprisonment within the body of a reptile was entirely another. She had only one option left. She had to eliminate Rose the Whyte before Ka wiped out millions.

"So El-on-ah," said Ka, continuing to study her intently. "Can I rely on you to do what needs to be done?"

Her answer came in a heartbeat, "Yes, My Lord, you can."

"Good, then I will send a list of instructions down for you presently. You are to locate the items listed and bring them to me at the Aureus Oratory, where I am to take up my rightful position as Prima Magister. From now on, every new ascendant will be schooled in accordance to *The Unification*. We are witnessing the birth of a new world El-on-ah, a better world, the world that we have long imagined, and you should take great pride in your role in its creation."

He rapped his fist on the door, three times. The guard swung it open, standing to attention as Ka made to leave.

"This ascendant is now in my employ. Provide her with whatever she needs."

El-on-ah caught the fleeting look of suspicion on the face of the guard, but even so, he was not foolish enough to question Ka's order, and El-on-ah was left alone.

Later, the guard reappeared carrying her occultus and two saddlebags crammed with supplies. Hesitantly she took them from him. Inside her occultus was a rolled parchment. She recognised the manuscript instantly from its gold scalloped edge. It was a single page ripped from a volume of *The Grimoire*, the rarest and most ancient book of magic known in the Afterlands. El-on-ah had only ever glimpsed its pages once before; there was a copy in the Oratory library, locked in a glass-fronted vitrine.

Her hands shook as she opened the parchment and as it unrolled, her potens ring slid into her hand. Hurriedly, she slipped it back on her finger letting out a long moan of relief. It was true what they said, separation from your potens ring was worse than losing a limb.

El-on-ah's eyes skimmed over the document's text. Each word was breathtakingly beautiful. Hand-illustrated letters were decorated with brightly coloured images, symbols, flowers and intricately drawn animals including dragons, leopards, and birds. The script outlined the procedure for brewing fractionation venom. The original print had been heavily annotated and El-on-ah had no trouble in recognising the hand.

Between the lines of the script and in all four margins, Lord Ka had carefully modified the confractio's original formula, together with much of the process of brewing and casting the charm.

El-on-ah shuddered as she read the list of ingredients, it was a recipe for evil, one tiny drop, enough to annihilate an entire city. Here in her hands, lay the means to commit the ultimate sin of war.

- CHAPTER EIGHT -

THE FAE

The journey to Kelpivale, though exhausting, had been relatively uneventful. Fatigue had long stifled their initial urge to indulge in friendly banter. Consequently, for the most part, the five of them walked in silence, focussing on what, for Rose, at least, was becoming an increasingly difficult task, the task of putting one foot in front of the other.

Initially, as they had made their way further west, the worst of the snow thawed and the afternoon sun, though hazy, had warmed their aching bones. That night had been more of a challenge. It fell quickly like a black cloud and brought with it a freezing mist. The hazy glitter softened the darkness but froze the ground to an icy glass that cracked beneath their feet.

As agreed, they had taken few breaks, just short stops to drink, eat, and rest their weary legs. They dared not risk lighting a fire. As the five of them trudged on into the early morning hours, the mist finally lifted, revealing the dark, inhospitable waters of Ogin's Deep. Speckles of soft light rippled across its surface, reflected glimmers of an enormous pale moon that grew larger and more translucent as dawn approached.

Attempting to keep within the cover of the overhanging crag, they had kept together in a tight line. Now, as they drew nearer to Kelpivale and the western coastline, Rose could taste the salt in the air, carried along by the Aborahs, Ferrum's legendary fierce onshore winds, which whipped at her face stinging her eyes and coating her skin with a thin powdery film.

The putrid aroma of rotting fish assaulted Rose's senses. She gagged. We must be nearing Kelpivale. She raised a small, tired smile at Sloley, who was, as usual, perched happily on Lee's shoulder. Periodically the loris flicked out his slender tongue, sampling the air before smacking his lips together and making curiously musical clicking noises as he savoured this salty treat.

Commander Linden slowed beside her, taking out his map.

"How much further to the Landings?" Rose, unusually impatient, didn't wait for his reply, "Will we be able to cross to Rhodium before dawn?"

"Maybe, if Ash has everything ready for us," said Linden, gesturing to a small finger-like outcrop ahead of them. "Once we round that ridge we should get a clear view of the Landings."

"Thank goodness," said Auriel, "I don't think these feet could carry me much further, they're killing me, and they'd probably ache even more if they weren't so frozen."

"They are not frozen Auriel," said Lee, "they may feel frozen, but truly, if they were frozen you then would be in serious trouble, and I doubt you'd still be walking. In fact, bits of them would probably have broken off by now."

"You know Lee," Auriel shook her head wearily, rolling her eyes skyward, "sometimes I have this almost irresistible urge to rip my ears off when you say things like that."

"Only sometimes?" Rose quipped.

Lee's brows arched dramatically, a hint of a smile flickered across his lips.

The cold wind intensified as they rounded the point and emerged from the shelter of the basin. It lashed at every inch of exposed skin, biting like a thousand tiny, needle-sharp teeth and leaving their cheeks stinging and raw. Up ahead of them Rose could just make out the Landings, an eclectic collection of ragged huts and wharfs, where local fishermen anchored their boats and landed their catches. Dawn was fast approaching; soon the whole area would be teeming with fishermen and their crew.

A figure emerged from behind one of the huts. Even from this distance, Rose recognised the tall, muscular silhouette framed in the moonlight, its bulky form implausibly lithe, like a dancing bear. Raising his arm, Ash motioned for them to join him. As Rose approached, she could see that Ash was not alone. Beside him stood a short, stout, bearded Ferrish native, dressed from head to toe in snow bear skin.

Squashed features protruded from a tangle of hair and fur. Rose found it hard to make out which belonged to him and which formerly, had been owned by the bear. The skin on his face was ruddy and weathered yet, beneath bushy brows, his eyes were the same vivid emerald green as Ash's. However, the most overwhelming impression the fisherman made on her was how strongly he smelled. He and in fact, the whole area, reeked of fish. The wooden jetty under their feet was slippery with ice, and frozen within it, sparkling like tiny pearlescent sequins, were thousands of fish scales interspersed with sinewy, grey lumps; fish guts yet to be taken by the gulls.

"I'm glad to see you all made it here safely," Ash welcomed them with a broad grin. His eyes flicked briefly to Rose as he rested a hand on the shoulder of the man at his side. "This here is Ewan, he's been fishing these waters for over thirty years, and he's agreed to take us across in his boat. To be fair, the man didn't take much persuading when he knew you would be with us Rose. You're quite a celebrity around these parts it seems."

Ewan barely lifted his eyes from Rose, except to cast a wary glance at the snow leopard circling soundlessly around them.

"It's good to meet you, Ewan, we appreciate your help," Rose offered her hand. "I expect Ash has relayed to you the importance of keeping our whereabouts from becoming widely known."

"Aye," said Ewan, rubbing his stumpy fingers on his coat before taking her hand. "Yea can rely on me and me lad, Lady Rose. We'll nay utter a word t' anyone. Yea can be assured o' that. 'Tis a real pleasure to meet you, so it is."

"Likewise, but please, call me Rose."

Ewan arched a brow, his eyes widening.

"We need to get going," Linden nodded towards the rapidly brightening eastern horizon.

"Everything is ready," Ash gestured to a heavily laden boat moored off the jetty. "We can depart right away. Isn't that right Ewan?"

"Aye," Ewan's eyes drifted nervously towards the large striped, white cat. "Though I'm nay sure about the…"

As he spoke, the snow leopard's form glowed, becoming blurred and indistinct. Flowing like warm jelly into an invisible mould it finally solidified, and Ro-eh-na stood before them.

"Is this more to your taste?" she asked.

"Oh, yeah, o' course… right," Evidently flustered Ewan averted his eyes from Ro-eh-na's deformed features. "I apologise, m' Lady, but we rarely see Ascendants in these 'ere parts an' I've never seen anyone do that. If ye follow me, I'll take yer bellow to yer accommodation. I doubt it's what yer used to, but it'll be warm an' dry, an' there's room enough t' rest yer bones."

Ewan's fishing schooner, expertly crafted from the finest Ferrish oak, was big enough to accommodate all of them comfortably. Below deck was a fair-sized chamber with a small galley. The room was furnished with a collection of mattresses, each strewn with colourful, hand woven blankets. Animal pelts covered the floor and a metal wood stove burned at the rear of the cabin where a pan of smoked fish soup simmered gently. By its side, a small table was laid with platters piled high with large slabs of fresh bread.

"Thank you, for going to all this trouble," said Rose.

"There's nay need t' thank us, me lady," said Ewan, "'Tis we that'll be thanking ye in the end I'll wager. Just make yer selves comfortable an' me an' the lad will get us underway."

Ewan's son, Oren, a small boy of about ten with an unruly head of chestnut brown hair, moved about them with the zeal of a whippet. Spooning large portions of the soup into pewter bowls, he handed one to each of them together with a wedge of fresh bread.

"Good lad," Ewan watched proudly from the steps of the cabin. "Now get thee on deck and raise the foresail."

"By me-self?" The boy's eyes widened excitedly.

"Aye," said Ewan with a wink, "special treat, I'll be up in a bit."

"Right ye are Da," Oren beamed as he clattered up the steps letting out a long, joyful whoop.

"You'd do well t' get some kip," Ewan gestured to the patchwork pillows resting on top of the mattresses. "Laurel, me wife, made those particular. All sorts in them, lavender, hops, lemon balm, rosemary and even a few rose petals I'll wager. Anyhows always does the trick fur me. Me head hits one of them an' I'm out like a candle in the Aborah. I'll be sure to wake yer before we make land."

Sitting on their mattresses, they warmed themselves by the stove before eating their simple meal. Linden unlatched the wood burner's small metal door and added a couple of logs before pulling on a long metal tab and opening up the flue. The fire to burst into life, filling the cabin with a soft glow and the homely smell of burning wood.

"Ewan's right," he said, "we should get some rest. I'm trained for this, and I'm about as tired as I've ever been. We'll need our wits about us when we reach Rhodium. Knuckers are not the only evil we will find there for sure."

"Evil... really? Is a wasp evil? Is a brown bear driven by wickedness?" Lee huffed indignantly, "knuckers are water dragons. That doesn't make them paragons of evil, it just makes them water dragons. In fact, as dragons they are quite fascinating, did you know that not only are they the only dragons that can survive under water and the only dragons that can't fly, but they're also the only ones unable to cast fyre. Knuckers are by far the most interesting of all of their phylogenetic class, furthermore..."

"I think I'm beginning to understand your 'tearing your ears off' remark earlier Auriel," said Linden with a chuckle.

"He does grow on you, though," Ash hitched up the side of his mouth, "...a bit like a fungus."

"I am still here you know," Lee flashed them a look of frustration. "I just don't see what's so evil about knuckers. They are simply animals that need treating with respect. They will only attack if you invade their territory or threaten their young. They're fish eaters for goodness sake!"

"As are sharks," said Auriel, "but Linden's right, it's not just knuckers we need to be concerned about. This area is known to be crawling with Fae."

"Fae?" Lee arched an eyebrow.

"According to *The Concise History of Rhodium: Foundation to Post Dragon War,*" Auriel closed her eyes as she read aloud from the virtual book, carefully stored in her mind, along with thousands of others. *"The Fae appeared after the Great Dragon War. Little is known of them, except for the fact that they are vaporous spirits of some kind. Never found south of Rhodium, Fae are generally confined to the areas surrounding Knucker Bay, Enisfrae and Dynasgwyn."* She hesitated momentarily, frowning. "It says here that if they pass through you, they freeze you solid. *Any interaction of this kind will kill a native instantly and can severely damage the bodies of ascendants, often irreparably."* Auriel opened her eyes. "That's why Rhodium has remained virtually deserted since the Great Dragon War. No one goes there now. No one sane that is..."

The cabin fell silent for a second until Ash noisily gulped down the last of his soup, mopping up the dregs with a large wedge of bread.

"Auriel, your knowledge never fails to depress," Ash wiped his mouth with his hand, glancing up at her and shaking his head with an exaggerated sigh. "Did you read every single book in the Oratory before we left?"

"Not every book," Auriel's eyes flashed indignantly, "just the ones that Lord Dux told me would be relevant." Her face clouded. "I hope that the Afreet didn't burn down the library. All of those manuscripts, all of that knowledge. Rose, you don't think…"

Rose did not answer. She lay, curled up on a mattress, head resting lightly on the sweetly aromatic pillow, her uneaten meal at her side.

"She's got it right, as usual," Ash pulled the thick woollen blanket over Rose's shoulders, "we should get some sleep."

Rose was awoken by the clatter of crockery, to the drone of tuneless whistling and the pungent smell of coffee.

Ewan stood in the small galley at the rear of the cabin. At first, Rose did not recognise him, nor the strangely furnished room, which seemed to lurch sickeningly, tilting sideways as she attempted to sit up. A wave of nausea washed over her.

"We'll be approaching land shortly, you'll feel a little better then," Ewan's face cracked into a knowing grin. "There's a wee jetty just ahead. I'll not be docking there, though; it's too risky. We'll anchor a little way offshore, and ye can take the small skiff. It'll take the six o' yer." Wavering for a second he added, "Any o' ye know how t' handle a skiff?"

"I can row," said Linden, "but what about our supplies?"

"Aye," said Ewan, "there'll be room enough for them too."

Rose forced down a mouthful of the freshly made coffee while she watched the others tuck into thick, salted biscuits spread liberally with some sort of fermented fish paste. Whatever it was it made her want to heave.

"Are you okay, Rose?" Ash said, "You look rather green."

"I'll be okay," Rose covered her mouth and nose with her hand, "I guess I'm that much of a sailor, and that smells awful. How can you eat that stuff?"

"You know us Muds, Rose," Ash said with a wink, "We have to eat to keep up our strength. You should try them, Kelpitats are a Ferrish delicacy."

"Not exactly fyrepot though is it?" Said Lee, "rotten fish with flour, salt, and water. Whatever inspired anyone to concoct something like that?"

"Starvation, I suspect," said Ash, "but you get used to the smell after a while and then they start to taste surprisingly good. Ewan tells me that the fishermen eat them to prevent sea sickness, so maybe you should try some Rose?"

"I'll pass thanks," said Rose, "I'm struggling to keep the coffee down."

She jumped at a sudden rushing, rattling sound. Ewan and Oren had dropped anchor and were releasing the skiff from its trusses at the stern of the boat. There followed a loud slap as the vessel hit the water. Waves pummelling the side of the boat, which rocked wildly for a few seconds. Oren held fast to the small craft's bow rope until the rocking had calmed when he tethered it tightly to the stern of the schooner.

"Good lad!" Ewan said, patting his son on one shoulder. "We'll make a fisherman of yer yet, so we will."

A few minutes later they were all on deck, their haversacks crammed with supplies. The air was needle-sharp. They pulled thick robes tightly about their bodies.

The wind had dropped to a zephyr. Nevertheless, the tiny ice crystals carried within it caused Rose's eyes prickle and tear. Blinking hard she pulled her hood over her face as she looked out towards the north. Expecting to see land, she groaned unconsciously as she saw only a thick white mist that eddied and flowed as the fickle breeze pulled it first this way, then that. The fog hung, suspended a few inches over the rippling water. It moved towards them like a ghostly apparition intent on swallowing them up.

"The fog will wane as the sun rises, I'd wait, but we're only a few hundred yards from shore now, it's over yonder, see you can just make out the shoreline." Ewan raised his arm, pointing out into the haze. Hesitating before adding guiltily, "I cannot risk taking yer any closer."

"That's fine Ewan," said Rose, aware of the sailor's increasing nervousness. "We appreciate you bringing us this far. I know that you would not usually venture this far into Rhodium, thank you and you also Orin."

Rose stifled a smile as the young boy flushed, averting his eyes.

As the six of them climbed down into the small skiff, it was evident that they would not all fit in safely. Their supplies took up almost half of the available space, and Linden took up most of what remained. Auriel slipped, landing uncomfortably on Linden's lap. Ash earned a stern glance from her when he failed to subdue a chuckle. Sobering, he turned to Ro-eh-na as they both attempted to maintain their footing on the cramped and very shaky deck. He linked his thumbs together, making a flapping gesture with his hands.

"Shall we?"

Ro-eh-na nodded. Ash's eyes flicked towards Rose.

"Good idea," she said, "but stay close to the boat, I don't want any of us out on our own around here."

Linden pushed off from the schooner, they lifted their hands in farewell but Ewan and Orin did not wait to bid them goodbye. The anchor had already been raised and the fishing boat had begun its journey back to Ferrum.

"Does anyone else get the feeling that they are rather keen to leave?" said Auriel, "I can't say that I blame them. It's rather creepy here isn't it?"

"Hardly," said Lee, "It's simply an advection fog caused by relatively warmer air flowing over the cold sea surface. I don't see why that should creep you out."

"No," said Auriel, "I don't suppose you would."

"I know what you mean Auriel," said Rose, the hairs on the back of her neck beginning to prickle, "there is something about it that makes my skin crawl."

Linden's massive, muscular arms moved decisively and rhythmically, lifting, dropping and then pulling the large oak oars through the water. The small boat moved quickly into the mist. Soon they were completely shrouded in its vast, suffocating void. The fog was so stiflingly opaque that it seemed to smother every sound. The eerie silence intensified until all that could be heard was the faint rhythmic swishing of the oars cutting through the water and the muffled beating wings of two white doves following closely as they edged ever nearer to Rhodium's concealed shoreline.

"What was that?" Auriel's voice was nervously hushed. "Did you hear that?"

"It's just the wind," said Lee.

"There's barely any wind," Rose's sense of foreboding was growing, "and even the Aborahs didn't howl like that."

"The Mud's call them the wailing Fae," Linden broke his stroke, letting the boat coast in the water as he turned his head towards the direction of the sound. "It is said that the day you hear the cry of the Fae, you'll not see nightfall."

"I doubt that there is a scrap of empirical evidence for that statement," said Lee, irritably "superstitious nonsense!"

"Auriel, have you read anything that could help?" Rose said, "Maybe you've heard of some spells that can be used to subdue them?"

"There are no spells that explicitly deal with the Fae, though blocking spells might work, I suppose." Said Auriel, "There is virtually nothing written about the Fae at all, so few people have ever survived a meeting. No one knows much about them, let alone how they are affected by magic. I don't think many ascendants have risked this journey and only a few Ferrish hunters have been desperate enough to brave this area. They visit only briefly, sailing across Ogin's Deep to trap snow bears for their pelts. I guess the promise of great wealth is enough to conquer a certain amount of fear. Of the few Muds who have encountered the Fae and lived to tell about it, all had managed to return to their boats before they were attacked. The Fae appear to be unable to cross the water."

Their boat emerged, gliding out of the mist like a bird soaring through the clouds into a sky full of sunlight. Rose gasped as she caught her first glimpse of Rhodium's desolate, snow-covered shoreline, looming before her in all of its grandeur. The magnificent glaciers of the Ice Mountains towered above them to the north and east. The morning sun glistened, crowning their glory as it ascended majestically behind their twin peaks, set against the backdrop of an endless topaz blue sky as if some divine artist had sketched in every inch of the scene ensuring each delicate point of colour was placed for maximum effect.

"It's beautiful," Rose's eyes began to smart. She felt bizarrely sentimental. This is my home. Though she had no recollection of the place so it was quite ridiculous that she should feel this way. This land of frozen snow was so dazzlingly white that it pained her eyes just to look at it and yet she could not stop looking, she took in every inch of it.

Now only a few feet from the shore, the mist hung behind them like a gleaming curtain flawlessly dividing water from land.

"Fascinating," Lee's eyes narrowed as he studied the phenomenon. He dipped his fingers into the water only to lift them out a second later, a smile of satisfaction lighting his face. "As I expected. The water is warmer here, which is why the advection fog is so thick just a few feet behind us while this area is clear. Still, I'm not sure why the water is so warm here considering all of the snow..."

"I think I can explain that," said Auriel, ignoring Lee's openly sceptical expression. "This area is geothermally active; it lies over the Rhodium plume, a volcanic hotspot. The mist over the warm water must be one of these geothermal effects, maybe the wailing we heard could be another?" This last question was asked with more than a hint of optimism.

"Possibly," Linden, grabbed for his quiver of arrows, placing them at his side before pulling hard on the oars and forcing the boat up into the shallows. "There's no harm in being prepared though is there?"

He manoeuvred the skiff towards the shoreline, weaving between large rocks that jutted from the water like an old giant's teeth; black, crooked and broken. There was no sign of the jetty that Ewan had described though Linden seemed unperturbed. When the water was around waist deep, Linden leapt over the side and guided the boat safely into the shore.

"Throw us the rope," Ash stood on the snowy bank with Ro-eh-na shivering uncomfortably at his side.

"Couldn't you have made that offer before I got into the water?" Linden tossed the line with such force that it knocked Ash backwards as he caught it.

"I guess I could have," Ash gathered up the slack and yanked hard on the cord, "but I just love watching you tough guys show off for the girls."

After landing the boat, they quickly gathered their supplies hitching the thickly woven haversacks up onto their shoulders.

"Which way now?" Linden grabbed up handfuls of the powdery snow, rubbing it over his wet limbs.

"Northwest, towards the Knucker holes," Rose arched her brows quizzically. "Linden, what are you doing?"

"It prevents frostbite," said Linden, "one of the things I picked up during cold weather training."

"Yeah," said Lee, with a quirk of his lips "like sticking your hand in the fire prevents burns…"

"What is that?" Ro-eh-na pointed a quivering hand towards the Northern horizon.

A dense, shimmering, silver-white fog was billowing up from the Northern snow lands and heading towards them at speed.

"A blizzard?" Linden squinted into the distance, "it looks like a snow storm though it seems remarkably localised."

"A blizzard… from a cloudless sky," said Lee, "really?"

They watched the swelling white cloud, in silence for a while, and then it began. A soft, pulsating, wailing cry, intensifying rapidly as the billowing miasma approached.

Sloley, suddenly agitated, let out a tirade of squeals and high-pitched clicks, as he frantically buried himself in the hood of Lee's cloak.

Cautiously, Linden unhitched the bow from his shoulder. Drawing an arrow from his quiver, in one seamless movement, he lifted his bow, set the arrow and took aim.

"Linden, I know I'm going to regret asking this," Lee glanced from Linden to the shimmering mist, now only a few hundred yards away from them. "But, what are you aiming at?"

"Whatever emerges from that," Linden jerked his head towards the fog.

The fog grew more opaque as it approached, glittering in the sunlight as millions of tiny crystals eddied and danced within the miasma.

"On your order Lady Rose." Said Linden.

A light breeze caught Rose's hair and it swirled around her like a silken cloak. Rose focussed her attention on the fog, which had stalled and was now billowing and shifting on the tundra about fifty yards ahead of them. She could see shapes moving within the miasma, tall, thin ghostly figures. These extraordinary, dynamic forms materialised, expanded and merged only to disperse and vanish seconds later.

Like the wings of some ethereal butterfly, the breeze caressed Rose's skin, bringing with it a familiar aroma. *Snow roses, I can smell snow roses.*

A form flew out from the approaching cloud. Letting out a long screech, it glided rapidly towards them like some ghostly eagle owl intent on their destruction. In an instant, Linden let fly his arrow.

"No!" Rose raised a hand towards the officer and then watched helplessly as the arrow flew past her towards the wraithlike figure.

The arrow hit, instantly freezing, it fractured, splintering into a thousand pieces, all readily absorbed into the glittering fog. The wailing intensified into a cacophony of blood-chilling screams. More figures began to emerge; soon there were hundreds of ghostly forms moving rapidly towards them.

The perfume of the snow roses was had grown intoxicating, suffocating, and yet at Rose felt no fear. Instead, there was a strange sense of calm, of belonging, as if she had reached her last refuge, her sanctuary.

"Wait there," her tone challenged any argument. "I know them, these are my people."

"Rose, you shouldn't go alone," Ash took hold of her arm, "let me..."

"I must do this alone," she placed her hand over his, "please Ash, I'll be okay. They will not harm me. These are my people Ash."

"Rose, we swore to protect you," said Ash "do not ask us to break our oath."

"I would never do that," She said, giving his arm a reassuring squeeze, "but if you accompany me you will be putting us both in danger."

"Please be careful Rose," he said, "I've kind of got used to having you around."

As Rose approached the emergent group of wraithlike creatures she did not look back. As she neared them, their wailing began to quieten. She could see them clearly now, transparent phantoms, peppered with ragged black holes, punched out from their substance like silver cobwebs shattered by stones. So this is what fractionation venom does; punctures the soul, ripping out its very essence. Before her were the remains of her people, the fragmented souls from whom Rose was ascended. These broken spirits were all that remained of the Whytes of Rhodium.

The snow crunched under her feet as she continued towards them and with each stride, the fragrance of snow roses grew more potent.

"It is she…" their hushed voices had a fragile, musical quality, "our redeemers are returned to us as we were promised. We have waited so long…"

Each word was carried along on the rose-scented breeze, the final words of each sentence fading, lost, towed away by the current of air.

One figure emerged from the assemblage. His lithe, vaporous form draped in long greyed robes. Though ragged and torn, Rose recognised them as the mantles of a Whyte ascendant. His long silver-white hair and beard hovered about him, covering much of his thin, deeply lined face. Then, as if caught in an underwater current, this silver veil of kelp drifted upwards, revealing a gaping black hole the size of a fist just below the cheekbone of one eye. Rose let out a sharp breath and halted in her tracks.

"We have waited long for you Rose of the Whyte," his words flowed like warm honey, melting quickly away as he spoke. "Are you well my dear friends?"

Friends? Rose turned, expecting to find that Ash had followed her, but she was alone. Ash stood watching her from where she had left him. She sensed his concern.

The wraith's eyes crinkled at their edges as he smiled, instantly reminding Rose of Lord Dux. She felt herself relax as a familiar warmth stirred within in her chest. It was the sensation experienced when greeting an old friend.

"Rose the Whyte, you may not remember me here," he placed a bony forefinger to his forehead, "but Ruzha, Ogin, Sevti and Eldwyn, they will remember me here." He set his hand flat at the centre of his chest.

"The four and I fought together during the Dragon War," he cast his eyes towards Ash and the others, who had endeavoured to move closer as they talked. His glare forced them to take a step backwards before his eyes returned to Rose. "You knew me as Gydion then. Now I come again to aid you, we ready ourselves for your call. You need only to speak my name."

"I wish that my memory of you was stronger Gydion, though I sense much warmth and I thank you for your offer of aid," said Rose," but at present my only aim is to locate a knucker."

"Knuckers abound in this area," Gydion hesitated, "though they do not take kindly to their eggs being plundered and we cannot protect you from their spew."

"We do not seek their eggs," said Rose, "and we are quite capable of defending ourselves."

"Ah, but it is not what you seek that is of concern," he gave a slow wink of an eye, "but that which seeks you."

A sudden squall blew up, seemingly from nowhere, lifting Gydion and his Fae high into the air, their forms disintegrating, scattering like snowflakes in a blizzard and returning them once more to the cloud of glittering dust that vanished as quickly as it had appeared.

Ahead of her now, the early morning sun lit the stark white landscape, dazzling her as she looked out on a seemingly endless expanse of snow-covered tundra.

"What did it say?" Ash cooed into Rose's ear.

She jumped, being unaware of his presence.

"His name is Gydion, he's an old friend," Rose, ignored Ash's questioning look, "he wanted to warn us to take care around the knuckers."

"Why does everyone have such a problem with knuckers?" Lee handed a piece of dried fruit to Sloley, who took it into his paws and nibbled at it eagerly. "Knuckers are only dragons and dragons are such unobjectionable animals."

"Yes, well you may revise your opinion after you have met one or two of them in the flesh."

"Never," said Lee, "Nothing can dampen my enthusiasm for such perfect animals. I mean, other dragons breathe out fyre but knuckers spew out ice. You have to admit that's cool.... Why are you all laughing?"

- CHAPTER NINE -

KNUCKERS

By late that afternoon, Rose's head was throbbing and she was convinced that each time they rested, someone had secretly stuffed stones into her haversack. Originally, she had intended to spend the journey time planning a safe strategy for obtaining knucker's spew. Instead, what she had done was listen to Auriel and Lee talk. Thankfully, as they reached the first of the Knucker Holes, they both quietened long enough to draw breath.

The small crater was like an inverted dome. Its lava-sculpted rim poked up from the surrounding ice, ejecting steam and bubbles like a cauldron of soup fit for a giant. Its sulphurous aroma was not so appetising. Rose held her breath in a predictably unsuccessful attempt at resisting her natural urge to breathe. It proved almost as futile as trying to avoid listening to Auriel recite every minuscule fact she had ever read about knuckers, which unusually, turned out not to be a whole lot. Even more strangely, Lee proved to be somewhat more of an expert, having read just about every book in the oratory library that even mentioned the word dragon.

"They'll be really overdue now," he said suddenly, cringing in dismay. "I've never failed to return a book on time before."

"Oh I wouldn't worry about that," Ash let his eyes flick to Auriel mischievously, "the whole library's probably gone up in smoke by now anyway."

"I don't think that is something you should be joking about," Auriel's lips set into a tight, thin line. "If that's true then all of our friends are probably gone as well."

"I am sure that they're not Auriel," Ash's smile faded. "I doubt that even Lord Ka and the Afreet can rid us of Lord Dux that effortlessly."

The four of them perched on the edge of the knucker hole, resting their feet and warming themselves on the heat from the rocks. Linden and Ro-eh-na sat opposite, on the other side of the rim. Linden's arm encircled Ro-eh-na's waist, supporting her securely as she dangled her feet over the hole and steeped them in the bubbling, steaming hot, mineral water.

"They seem to be getting very friendly," Ash tossed a suggestive wink towards Rose. "I thought fraternisation between casts was forbidden, let alone ascendant and native. Won't they grow two heads or something?"

Rose studied the couple for a while; they looked so carefree as they kicked their feet in the water, playfully splashing one other. She felt her face relax into a smile. *What must it be like to feel that way?*

"That kind of bigoted belief system is in the past now," the wistful smile dropped from her lips as she continued to watch them, "at least I hope it is."

"You know," A flash of insight brightened Auriel's eyes. She leant over, dipping her hand into the briny blue liquid. Sheepishly she cast a glance in Rose's direction. "I can't remember the last time I had a bath..."

"Well, I did say we would rest when we got here." Rose mirrored Auriel's air of conspiracy, the thought of immersing herself in the warm salty liquid was extremely tempting, "and I can't think of a better way to relax."

Then, letting out loud whoops, they threw off their outer robes and leapt into the foaming, blue water. The brine sprang up like the glistening tails of a hundred tiny porpoises, splattering Lee and Ash's astonished faces and transforming Sloley into a woolly pinecone, his fur clumping together in a collection of damp brown tufts.

Ash and Lee regarded each other with wide eyes as water dripped from their hair. Then, hooting with laughter, they discarded their wet clothing and dove into the water.

The briny water effortlessly supported Rose's slight frame. She floated, gazing up into the cloudless sky and moaning with pleasure as thousands of tiny bubbles pummelled at her body. Steam rose around her. This feels so good, she thought, even if it does stink.

"This is absolute bliss," Auriel smiled up at the pair sitting at the edge of the pool. "You should join us Ro-eh-na, it's wonderfully warm, it would be so soothing for your..."

"No," Ro-eh-na's body tensed, her relaxed manner vanishing. She shook her head, drawing her cloak tightly around her, "I'm quite happy just warming my feet... thanks."

No one spoke for a while then. Auriel seemed utterly dismayed. Rose could sympathise, they had both grown used to the scars on Ro-eh-na's face but chosen to forget that her wounds did not stop there.

"Ro-eh-na, you can still join them," Linden whispered into her ear, giving her arm a reassuring squeeze. "I believe seals are quite at home in water."

Rewarding him with a beautifully crooked smile Ro-eh-na's striking almond eyes brimmed and glowed, instantly liquefying as they transformed into the limpid black eyes of a sleek grey seal. With smooth gracefulness, the animal slid from his arms and into the water.

Laughter rang out as Ro-eh-na cut through the water, effortlessly rolling and weaving between them.

"You too Linden," Ash gestured for him to join them.

"Not right at this moment, thank you," Linden held up his hands, shaking his head. "Maybe it would be prudent for at least one of us to remain dressed and on solid ground."

Pulling on his boots, Linden gathered up his belongings and went to sit on a large boulder, which provided him with an expansive view of the tundra. Taking a strip of deer jerky from his pack, he chewed on it as he watched them, smiling with a relaxed air of contentment.

Rose tipped back in the warm water, her silver-white hair fanning out like an unruly halo. She closed her eyes, revelling in the sensations that pervaded her body as the effervescent, pulsating jets of bubbles kneaded and soothed her tired, aching muscles. There was something very gratifying about bathing amidst the snow and ice, the cold breeze sharp in your face as your body tingles with the caress of a thousand fizzing eddies.

Submerging herself entirely under the surface of the water Rose rubbed her face with her hands before emerging, pushing her wet hair out of her eyes and gazing out over the tundra. Seven stone boulders stood erect, like ancient monoliths, casting giant shadows as the mid-afternoon sun dropped ever lower in the azure sky. The cold air sent a sudden chill through her wet skin.

"Sorry everyone," Rose said, hating that she had to drag everyone back to reality, "but we should eat and then get going. We need to be out of the Knucker Holes by nightfall, and we've yet to find a way inside."

"Well, that shouldn't be difficult should it," Lee's eyes shifted markedly to Sloley, who, snuggled amidst Lee's discarded clothes, had begun preening himself meticulously. "After all, we do have one of the most expert foragers in all of the Afterlands with us."

"Okay then," Ash looked at the others as they bobbed in the water with only their faces exposed to the freezing cold air, "so who's going to get out first?"

"I was first in, so I'll get out and heat up a rock or two," Rose swung herself up onto the edge of the crater.

Rose didn't feel the effects of the cold as the others anyway. Grabbing her robes, she wrapped her cloak about her body and slipped on her pumps. Selecting the largest of the seven boulders, Rose placed her palm above its speckled granite-like surface.

"Incendium"

A fiery, silver light crackled and leapt from her ring, its pulsating glow enveloping the massive monolith. As the boulder warmed the snow melted rapidly around it. Rivulets of water trickled away, fleeing from the growing heat.

They sat, wrapped in their cloaks as they ate. Rose watched them, prodding and teasing each other, laughing through chattering teeth as they waited for their clothes to dry. *I have all the warmth I need right here.*

Once dressed, newly warmed and invigorated, the group were in high spirits and eager to begin the next stage of their journey. Lee and Sloley were on point, travelling due north, across the desolate, frozen tundra and out towards the southwestern peninsula of Knucker Bay.

Rose marvelled at their bond, they seemed so perfectly in tune with one another. Periodically, Sloley stretched out his short neck, nose twitching vigorously and his tongue tasting the air. This was the signal for Lee to pause, and concentrate on the tirade of seemingly incomprehensible chirping and chattering emanating from the tiny creature, before subtly, but decisively, readjusting his route.

Less than an hour later Sloley made a discovery. The little Loris grew extremely agitated, his muted chatters transforming into high pitched squeals as he leapt from one shoulder to the other, circling Lee's head, spinning around it like a fur covered top.

"There are Knuckers ahead of us," said Lee, "Sloley's a little concerned about this though I don't see why…"

"Yeah, we know," Ash mimicked Lee's dispassionate tone, "because they're only dragons, and just like other animals they aren't evil, we've no reason at all to be scared of dragons…"

Lee narrowed his eyes.

"You know," Lee's lips twisted into something vaguely resembling a smile, "I find it really encouraging that you are learning so much from me. Keep it up and one day you may just make a C in Cognito after all."

He lifted Sloley from his shoulder and giving him a reassuring pat, he stuffed him safely away inside his backpack.

"If Sloley is correct," Lee waved his arm towards a small rise up ahead of them, "then that hill is not a hill at all, but the walls of a massive knucker crater with an entrance to the knucker holes."

"However can he know that?" Linden's brow furrowed as he looked at the nondescript, snow covered mound ahead of them.

"Well," Ash, slapped a hand on Lindens shoulder. "Let's just say that Sloely makes up for his lack of taste in best buddies by having the capability to locate a grape, wrapped in garlic, encased in a lead box, buried in a sack of compost and hidden at the bottom of the deepest mine in Hydrargyrum. All with a few twitches of that tiny snout."

The top of the mound did indeed turn out to be the edge of large knucker hole. Linden eyed it with a look of trepidation. The rim of the crater was narrow, about a foot's width of fresh snow rested on inch thick ice. Its sides were steep and smooth, like a giant china breakfast bowl and there, about fifty feet below them at its centre was a dark, rounded fissure.

"That can't be the entrance," Linden's brows furrowed, "I doubt that even I could fit through there, let alone a full grown knucker. Anyway, we'd be crazy to try and climb down; it's pretty much sheer ice."

"I agree," Lee's body tensed, his feet slipping on the uneven ground. "It's difficult enough trying to keep upright here, particularly when you've got crazy animal jiggling about on your shoulder."

Sloley was now perched precariously on the back of his neck. His tiny paws gripped Lee's hair, yanking back his head.

"For goodness sake, Sloley," Lee flung out his arms, flailing them about like a windmill, "keep still you'll have us both off..."

Lees attempt at counterbalancing exacerbated the situation drastically, his feet slipped from under him and the pair toppled over the edge of the rim.

"Noooooo... " Lee's cries echoed around the giant amphitheatre.

"Well that's one way of getting down there I suppose," said Ash, with a grin as he watched them slide down the side of the crater towards the black crevice at its centre, "you can always count on Lee to find a novel solution to our problems. Shall we join them?"

Rose's eyes widened, travelling from Ash's amused expression, down the grooves on the side of the basin and to the wailing figure now fast disappearing into the hole at the centre of the crater.

"You have to admit it Rose that looks unbelievably good fun," Ash lowered himself eagerly onto the edge of the crater, "last one down's a stink hole..."

Not waiting for Rose's approval he pushed himself off, raising his arms above his head as he slid rapidly down the incline.

"Whooo.... Guys... you've... got... to... try... this... it's... bloody... AWE... SOME...."

"Shall we?" Rose's lips hitched in a wry smile as she tossed a glance at Auriel, offering her hand.

"I can't believe we are doing this," Auriel hesitated, then shrugged, grabbing Rose's wrist she pulled her off her feet.

Rose shrieked as the pair slipped into a natural furrow in the ice and hurtled down the sides of the slope. As they neared the opening of the knucker hole, they let out a stream of nervous laughter.

"This is just madness," Linden shook his head as he watched their descent, "there's no way…"

"Surely you are not afraid Commander Linden?" Ro-eh-na teased, "you'll fit through fine, the opening is much bigger than it looks from up here."

"We have no idea what is at the bottom," said Linden, "we could be sliding into the open mouth of a dragon for all we know."

"You're worried about been eaten by knuckers?" Ro-eh-na laughed, "The fall will probably kill us!"

She nudged Linden playfully in the back. Instinctively he stuck out his arms, overbalancing. Then he tipped forward and plunged headfirst down the icy bank. Chuckling, Ro-eh-na crouched at the edge of the crater, before transforming once more into the guise of a snow leopard. The huge cat sidled forward, then followed him down, with its four giant paws spread out like a gawky fawn and its tail held erect, waving about like the rudder of a ghost ship.

Ro-eh-na had been right, the fissure was much larger than it had appeared from above, though, and it was far from the end of their descent. Once inside, they found themselves whooshing along an extended tube-like tunnel, its walls packed with thick, glassy ice. Slowing a little as the incline decreased, they continued to descend deep underground. Twisting and turning, coiling and spinning, the tunnel echoed with cries of uneasy laughter, playful excitement and intermittent terror.

Eventually, the chute came to an abrupt end, suspended about six feet above the floor of an immense, underground cavern. They tumbled out one by one, landing in a heap onto a mound of powdery snow.

Prisms of ice, like giant shards of glass, spiked from the ceilings and walls, scattering the available light into hundreds of rainbow-coloured beams that sparkled and bounced around the cave.

"Move... quickly!" yelled Ash, pulling Lee out from under him, "Linden's on his way down."

"And... you're afraid that he may land on top of me like you just did?" Lee huffed, getting to his feet, brushing snow from his robe and patting at his hood.

"Oh no..." Lee's eyes frantically scoured the mound of disturbed snow.

"What's up?" asked Ash.

Screams of excitement, growing rapidly in volume, drifted down from the chute above.

"Sloley's gone. I can't see him anywhere, can you?" Lee's voice trembled.

Just then, Rose and Auriel dropped out of the chute, falling just front of him, laughing hysterically, their faces flushed.

Ash grabbed their arms, pulling them clear barely a second before Linden came crashing down, followed by the wettest most bedraggled looking cat imaginable.

Ro-eh-na landed heavily on Lindens upper body, winding him badly. Righting herself, she shook her coat, splattering all of them with foul, leopard-scented drool.

Their protests were stifled by Lee's urgent voice.

"Ro-eh-na, we can't find Sloley. Can you help?"

The cat's dark eyes blinked in response as she raised her nose into the air. Instantly she caught a scent, spinning around she bounded over Linden's prone body. Four massive paws padded soundlessly towards a small pile of snow thrown up by their arrival. The cat buried her muzzle deep into its powdery mass until the icy granules invaded its nostrils prompting an enormous sneeze, which blew away the snow and revealed a wet, shivering, bundle of fur.

"Sloley," Lee fell to his knees beside the tiny animal, "are you okay?"

The trembling bundle unfurled. Two enormous, saucer-like eyes narrowed, fixing accusingly on the young Alchemist.

"Oh, come on Sloley," Ash rested a hand on Lee's shoulder, "don't give Lee such a hard time, things could have been so much worse... the cat could have landed on you."

"Or even worse than that," Ro-eh-na had transformed back into her Ascendant form, her lips slanted in a quirky smile, "it could have been Linden."

"Oh, I'm not sure that would have been worse," Linden spluttered, slapping his chest as he attempted to get to his feet. He leant forward briefly with his hands on his knees, taking a long breath before finally pulling himself up to his full height. He quickly discovered that this was a mistake, as he cracked his head on a gigantic stalactite hanging from the roof of the cavern.

"It's just not your day, is it?" quipped Ash

"This place..." Auriel's jaw dropped, "it's like a cluster of rainbows trapped in a crystal ball."

"Yes, it is... unbelievably beautiful," but Rose wasn't looking at the cave, she was watching Lee, tenderly lifting the tiny Loris and carefully checking each of his fragile limbs before wrapping him gently in his cloak.

"Don't scare us like that again will you," Lee moved his lips, brushing Sloley's ear, "I've grown to kind of... rely on you now, and besides Rose needs you. You're a valuable member of our team you know, so... where to next?"

Sloley nudged his head towards and opening at the far side of the cavern, making three small clicks with his tongue before burying his face in the crook of Lee's arm.

"Through there," Lee deposited Sloley gently into his hood, arranging the thick black material carefully around him. "If you are still intent on locating knuckers, you will need to take that passageway."

"Luceat Lux," Rose spoke the illumination incantation quickly as she made her way over to the tunnel entrance, the others following closely behind.

The crystal in her potens ring shone brightly, illuminating the passage as they ventured inside. The walls of the passage were coated with a thick vivid blue substance. Rose brushed the tips of her fingers over it and gathered a layer of sticky blue slime.

"That looks gross… it smells gross too," said Ash, adding hesitantly, "Rose, don't you think that maybe it's time you told us what we're looking for? If you let us help you, we'll have a much better chance of finding it."

Pausing, Rose brought their procession to a brief halt. Rose knew he was right, but they had trusted Lord Baroque and had even let El-on-ah into their circle, with disastrous results. Can she risk being wrong again?

"Okay," Rose bit down on her lip as she turned to face them. "Ash is right, we're a team and if we cannot rely on each other, what are we fighting for anyway? So, here it is. When the Incantatio spoke, it urged me to seek out 'Ice that stays the heat of fyre' which apparently, I should then store in knucker's spew. I have no idea what either of those things is but I knew I needed to find knuckers, so here we are. Any ideas?"

"Really... You don't know what knucker's spew is... None of you?" Lee shot a questioning look at Auriel's blank expression and let out an exaggerated gasp of exasperation. "Well, whatever do they teach you Memorix in Cognito classes these days? Knucker's spew is the breath of an ice dragon of course. Fyre dragons breathe out fyre and ice dragons breathe out…"

"Ice?" ventured Ash.

"Oh really," said Lee, with sigh "Spew of course! It has the properties of both liquid and gas. It freezes whatever it touches instantly, preserving it forever, or until it is disturbed. It makes matter so fragile that the slightest amount of pressure will cause it to splinter into millions of tiny pieces."

"So the Incantatio instructed Rose to preserve ice inside something that turns everything into ice?" Ash shrugged. "That just doesn't make sense at all, or am I missing something?"

"Invariably," said Lee, his lips twitching involuntarily.

"Okay Lee, I don't think any of us would argue that you are smart. You know everything there is to know about dragons," Auriel's tone was smug, "but how is it that you, an Alchemist, appear to have never heard of the one substance capable of 'staying the heat of fyre'?"

"Oh, this just gets better and better," said Ash, "I take it from that Auriel, that you do know the name of this elusive substance?"

"I do... It is known as diamond dust." Auriel's eyes glinted in amusement as Lee's chin jutted out so far she could have hung a kettle from it. "Whatever do they teach you in Alchemy classes these days?"

"Touché..." Ash touched his forehead in mock salute. "So what is it and how do we find it?"

"It's a vapour, a foggy mist formed in bright, clear skies at very low temperatures. It's made up from tiny ice crystals and its beauty is said to astound you. Though goodness knows how we are going to collect it."

"So that must be why we need the knucker's spew, to preserve the particles of diamond dust and keep them separated." Said Rose, "That means we'll need to collect the spew first. So now, all we need to do is find a knucker."

"You do know, despite what Lee says, those things are extremely dangerous," said Ash, "I mean seriously how…"

"Hold on," Linden's hushed voice boomed in the small tunnel. "I think I may know where we can find the diamond dust."

"You do?" Lee's brows arched dramatically, "then maybe you should major in Cognito instead of Auriel…"

"Shush," said Auriel, "maybe you should major in bad manners! Go to Linden."

"When we first encountered the Fae on the tundra," he hesitated, "I may be wrong but weren't they surrounded by a fog just like that."

"Yes, they were…" Rose recalled the wraith-like figures floating in a thick bright mist, speckled with a million tiny shards of light, "you are right Linden, it was exactly like that. I can summon the Fae when we have the spew."

"You know how to do that?"Ash raised his brows as Rose nodded. "So what do you do, did they give you a horn to blow or something?"

He jumped as an ear-splitting blast, something between a roar, a howl and a scream sounded from deep inside the tunnel.

"Now that… is a knucker," Lee's eyes widened, "magnificent isn't it?"

"Man, if you think that sounds like something good," Ash shook his head, "then being a nerd is the least of your problems."

"Lee, as our resident expert on knuckers," Rose ignored the twinkle of amusement in Ash's eyes. She cleared her throat, "have you any idea how we might harvest their spew?"

Lee unclipped the clasp on his occultus, rummaged inside and brought out a glass specimen jar with a large cork bung in the top.

"This should be quite adequate for what we need."

"Of course," said Ash, "I see your intention now. We just have to encourage the knucker to spit in the jar... why didn't I think of that? Oh, I know because it's a stupid plan that's why."

"Evidently," said Lee, "that is why you thought of it. No, we'll need to use magic, and there is only one of us here who has the skill."

"I would have to cast a block and a holding spell simultaneously, wouldn't I?" Rose felt their eyes resting on her like lead weights. "I've not done that before..."

"It won't be safe, Rose. There isn't enough room in these tunnels; it wouldn't give you enough time. Unless..." Ash turned to Lee, "Everything fears something, right? So what do knuckers fear?"

"The adults have no natural predators if that's what you mean," Lee's eyes flashed with sudden insight, "but, they absolutely detest snow foxes. It's on account of them being rather partial to knucker eggs. Why, what are you suggesting?"

"I am suggesting that you all return to the cavern. I'll transform into a snow fox, locate the beast and lure it out. Rose, you can wait in the cavern at the tunnel entrance. It will give you an element of surprise and you'll have all the space and time you'll need. I think it could work, all I'd have to do is annoy the knucker enough to get it to chase me."

"Even though, being an Ascendant, the animal's poison won't harm you," said Lee, "and annoying the beast should be absolutely no problem, especially for you. Knuckers are extremely fast and its spew hits you, you will literally be iced."

"Literally?" said Ash.

"Literally," Lee's expression did not alter, "then, even the slightest amount of pressure will cause fractures. Even if we found a way to thaw you out, I'm not sure you'd be able to morph yourself back from that without at least missing one significant body part."

"He'd stand a better chance if I went along as well," said Ro-eh-na, "two of us should be able to entice the beast while at the same time confusing it enough to stop either of us becoming permafrost."

"You are assuming that there is only one of them, what if there are more," Linden grasped Ro-eh-na's wrist, jerking her towards him. "Is it not enough that you almost burned to death, now you want to risk being frozen for eternity?"

"I would risk that and more," Ro-eh-na's eyes flashed boldly, "much more if it means defeating Ka and the scum he freed from Erebus, and so would you Commander."

They all knew that she was right and Linden did not argue.

"It's a viable plan and we have little else," Rose threw a cautious glance towards Ash, "but please take care, we are few as it is, and I do not think I could cope with losing any more of my friends."

The knucker roared once more. This time, it was much closer and moving towards them.

"It's caught our scent," said Lee, "If we're going, we need to go now."

"Ready?" Ash turned to Ro-eh-na taking her hand.

Instantly their bodies dissolved into shimmering, elastic figures that warped and constricted, reforming into small, white foxes. Racing ahead, they quickly disappeared into the darkness.

The others returned to the cavern and Rose took up a position at its centre and directly opposite the entrance to the passageway.

"You will need to remain behind me," as she spoke, Rose's gaze never wavered from the tunnels craggy entrance. "It's the only way I can protect you."

As if challenging those words, a monstrous roar filled the cavern and the thundering of massive limbs shook the ground beneath their feet.

"Behind me, NOW." Rose, spread her arms protectively.

A small white fox shot from the tunnel entrance, darting sideways and just avoiding a jet of cobalt coloured liquid and vapour. It hit the wall of the cavern, freezing instantly into a layer of thick blue ice. Losing its footing the fox slid sideways into a large boulder beside Rose. Instinctively, she ran forward towards the gigantic, blue scaled beast as it burst through the too small opening, scattering rock and ice before it. The walls rumbled and shook around them.

Piercing yellow eyes fixed on Rose as the animal drew back its head, opened its jaws and ejected a thick stream of spew towards her.

"Obsepio," Rose cast the blocking spell, moving instantly into a blocking action and sending a wall of white energy flying towards the spew and obstructing its path. *"Tenere,"* Without a second's hesitation she screamed the holding command.

Time stilled. The dragon and its stream of icy blue spew hung motionless in the air.

Lee moved forward tentatively, lifting the specimen jar, he scooped up a large globule of spew and carefully replaced the lid.

Linden rushed to the side of the fox as it began to transform.

"Hey Linden," Ash greeted him with a wry smile, "I didn't know you cared..."

"Where's Ro-eh-na?" Linden did not attempt to hide his concern.

"Yeah," said Ash, rubbing his head, "I'd rather like to know the answer to that question myself, as she just upped and left me to it."

"She'd never do that," Linden's face reddened.

"Well, she did. If you don't believe me, why don't you ask her yourself?" Ash jerked his head towards the small white fox as it ran out of the passage and towards Rose.

Between its jaws, it carried a smooth oval object emitting a soft green glow. Ro-eh-na dropped it at Rose's feet as she rematerialized.

"I think it's part of the incantatio," Ro-eh-na said, catching her breath. "It's a fossilised knucker's egg. I found it in a small chamber off one of the passageways. I'm sorry I left you Ash, but if you had not distracted the knucker, I would never have been able to take it."

"It is the incantatio," Rose lifted the egg from the ground, it blazed like a captured star, "and I think you have all earned the right to see its magic revealed. Stand back everyone."

Placing her ringed hand over the stone Rose spoke the incantation.

"incantatio secretum tuum,"

The rock exploded in a blaze of emerald light, bursting open like a fiery puffball. Shimmering, molten silver letters floated in the air, aligning to form a quivering script that danced before them.

An icy curtain holds the key,
Spectra trapped for eternity,
Break one finger of silver hue,
And lay this down in knuckers spew.
The charms requirements,
One half met,
Complete in one final piece.
Should you dare to collect.

"It's telling us where we need to go next," said Auriel, "the icy curtain. It can only mean the frozen falls, and they are right between here and Isingwilde."

"It also tells us what we need to collect," Lee would not be outdone, "the finger of silver hue has to be antimony, it's a rare silver grey mineral, the grains get washed down from the mountains and become trapped in the ice. It makes sense that you'd need antimony for your charm, it has the property of repelling fyre."

"Lord Eldwyn has planned this all so meticulously," Auriel shook her head. "All those thousands of years ago, how could he predict all this, our arrival, our every move?"

"The incredible power of magic," Rose felt the strength of the potens ebbing and flowing within her. A tidal wave of energy, primed and ready to be channelled. "It is such an amazing gift. Don't you see how it connects us all, those that have gone before and those yet to come? It draws us to our destiny and provides us with the power to realise it."

"You talk as if it's alive," said Ash.

"It's more alive than we are. We are merely its vessels. Take away our physical bodies and we are all Fae. Each one of us afloat on a sea of magical energy, drawing our power from the one timeless, omniscient conduit, even Lord Ka."

"That's a scary thought," said Ash, "I don't fancy being in the same boat as him, not with Lord Eldwyn plotting the course. The incantatio may have provided us with clues, but it held a warning too, or was I the only one to notice?"

"Oh, I think we all noticed," said Lee.

"Well, unless we get out of here soon, we won't have to worry about that," said Auriel, casting her eyes back towards the dragon, "magic is notoriously short-lived when it's used against knuckers."

A yellow eye swivelled in its socket, following them out as they left.

- CHAPTER TEN -

DIAMOND DUST

Climbing out of the knucker hole was no easy task. Sloley's nose led them to an opening in one of the tunnels. The light from the crevice streamed out into the darkness like a message from the heavens, *follow me and you will be saved.* Though spacious enough to crawl through initially, the gap narrowed rapidly as they climbed until Linden struggled to continue. However, as the tunnel steepened he was able to use his bulk and strength to push his way up to the surface. Once out he let down the rope and effortlessly pulled the others up to join him.

The sun had all but set. A smudge of amber on the horizon the only indication of its passing. The temperature had dropped markedly. Rose did not feel the effects of the cold, but the others gathered their cloaks tightly around themselves, blowing into cupped hands and vigorously stamping their feet.

As she watched them, Rose stepped up onto a small rise. The freezing wind whipped at her cloak and it billowed out behind her caressing her quivering mantle of silver-white hair.

"I'm going to call the Fae," she said, peering ahead into the snowy tundra.

The soft white snow of the open tundra had shifted, dimming into a kaleidoscope of infinite grey hues.

"We need the diamond dust and though you are the Alchemist Lee, I think it would be wise if I collected it alone," Rose knew the Fae did not care for Bloods, and who could blame them, had it not been a Blood that had damned them to eternal purgatory.

Lee nodded, without speaking, though she wondered if this affirmation was merely an exaggeration of his violent shivering. Lee withdrew a trembling hand from the warmth of his cloak and handed Rose the flask of knucker spew.

"Hey there buddy," said Ash with a grin, "no need to be so anxious, I'll protect you."

Lee drew his arm back inside his cloak, wrapping it tightly around his body.

"I need to get warm, I am literally freezing," his voice was shaking almost as much the rest of his body.

"Really," said Ash, quirking an eyebrow, "literally?"

Rose pointed to a circle of large boulders a few hundred yards away.

"There," she said, "the pillars should give us some shelter from the wind. Heat up one of the rocks and we'll camp there for the night. I'll join you when I'm done."

"Rose, you're not meeting the Fae alone?" said Ash.

"They did me no harm earlier Ash and they won't now either. I'll be okay," Rose felt a strange fluttering in her chest as she caught his look of concern and she found herself paying unusually close attention to his expression.

"…and you are confident of that because?" His voice wavered slightly, his eyes avoiding her gaze.

She found herself smiling.

"I just am…" she murmured, "I promise you have nothing to fear. I must do this alone Ash."

She placed a hand lightly on his arm before leaving him to climb to the summit of the small knoll about a hundred feet above the knucker hole.

Rose struggled more with each step, the deep snow clawing at her robes as she walked. She felt Ash's eyes on her for a long while, until she was swallowed up by the descending greyness. Suddenly Rose felt very alone.

When she reached the summit, looking out over the broad expanse of tundra, Rose could make out little but sporadic patches of grey and white shrouded in shadow. Raising her arms, like a delicately carved figurehead at the bow of a ship, she leant forward against the wind, her silver hair streaming out behind.

"I call on you, my kith and kin," Rose shouted the words, but they were taken instantly by the wind, "I beseech you, my family, to come to me, come here to me now…"

The wind whistled about her, stifling her words and scattering their vestiges across the tundra. She felt dejected. How can they possibly hear me, they could be hundreds of miles away by now. Cupping her hands around her mouth, she called out once more, and again. Then, as suddenly as before, the scent of snow roses filled her senses as she watched the glistening white cloud approaching through the darkness. Like one enormous entity, it billowed forward, travelling rapidly and against the direction of the wind.

Then Gydion was before her, ahead of the bank of swirling mist, hovering a few feet above the snow, in all his ethereal majesty.

"Rose of the Whyte," his words were crystal, chiming in the air, impervious to the winds attempt to carry them off. "I did not expect you to hear from you so soon my friends. What can we do for you?"

Rose waivered, she would never get used to being addressed as an assemblage. To Rose, the four souls she carried were indistinguishable from herself. They were one. Not to Gydion, it would seem.

"Gydion, we apologise for disturbing you my friend," said Rose, thinking that it could do little harm to humour him, "but I… we, need to acquire some diamond dust, and we believe you may be able to provide us with some."

"Indeed," he said, "have you an appropriate substrate in which to store it?"

Rose held out the flask.

"Knucker's spew?" he asked, "I am encouraged to see that you have retained your audacity and your expertise, my friends. In which case…"

Gydion waved a bony hand towards the curling white cloud, his tattered sleeve flailing in the air as he let out a piercing wail, the shrill sound making her ears buzz and pop. Wincing, Rose pressed her palms hard against them.

The haze responded immediately. It billowed out towards them until it drew close enough for Rose to see the ocean of wraithlike faces gazing out. There were hundreds of them, each ghostly, broken soul soared and dived within the glittering mist like a brood of jellyfish buoyed along on a star spangled sea. Then the fog engulfed them and an all-consuming sense of dread descended on her, *'if they pass through you, they freeze you solid'*.

The miasma swirled around her, suffocating her with its intoxicating fragrance, the shrill howling of its quickening, turbulent current deafening her ears. Thousands of glittering particles stung her face, catching in her hair and frosting her lashes. Her head swam, as with each icy breath she sucked the frosted dust deeper into her lungs until she could inhale no more. Sounds faded to a distant hum. She felt no pain, no fear, nothing but the isolation of eternal purgatory. *Whatever we may like to think, ultimately, we are all on our own.*

Staring at the shimmering aura with unblinking eyes, Rose became mesmerised by the rhythmic eddying of the icy crystals as they floated around her. *Beautiful...* her last thought, as consciousness finally escaped her and her lids fluttered closed.

Frosted lashes, expanding like blossoming feathers, tickled her skin, awakening her senses. A window opened and the world burst upon her once more. Sensations flooded back, each wave pushing her, invigorating her; *wake up,* shouted the blast of icy cold, *wake up,* the maelstrom whistled all around her, *arise with me,* beckoned the scent of white roses.

Forcing open her eyes, Rose willed them to focus; to look past the mist and into the faces of the Fae. They were all around her, soaring above her, crowding in. Rose saw her terror reflected in their glassy eyes. She sensed something; rage, envy, love, hate... sorrow? The intense aura of conflicting emotions unnerved her, but she could not afford to be distracted from her purpose.

Uncapping the flask of spew Rose drew the mouth of the jar through the air, capturing millions of glistening particles. She secured the bung, slipping the phial into her occultus; her hands trembled as she fastened the straps.

The heavily scented miasma grew denser, as the Fae drew ever closer, their cold breath on her skin. Her heart fluttered like a caged bird. *Where are you when I need you?*

They were with her almost instantly, their words bursting from her like birdsong, the unfamiliar sounds uttered instinctively, without memory or thought.

"We are Rose the Whyte," a choir of voices rang out into the whistling, swirling mist. "We are Ruzha, Ogin, Sevti and Eldwyn and we remember you. We remember you Myza, Lilith, Ocra, Levin and Sergin. We remember you Beni, Glynith, Sami... Phedra... We remember you, and we know well the evil that brought you here. We return to settle the great debt that is owed to you. Time will come when together we will take back our lands, rid our world of Djinn and restore sovereignty to the Afterlands. Until then, we ask for your patience, and your allegiance. Rhodium is our land, we will return to take our place once more in this world, and our spirits will be restored."

Gaunt faces closed in on her, barely a breath away, their vacant eyes burning into her. Rose could not find her breath. *If they stretched out their fingers, they could finish me now.*

The wailing maelstrom intensified, whirling around her, twisting her cloak around her body, wrapping her so tightly that she could barely move. One by one the figures twirled, rising above her like cinders, ragged wafers of charred paper buoyed along on the current. As the cloud lifted and moved away, their wailing cries grew indistinct.

'When you call us, we will come..."

A thousand years ago, they had believed that the four great wizards of Rhodium would protect them. Eldwyn had let them down. Where do they find the faith to trust again?

"This time, it will be different," she whispered.

"That is indeed good to hear," Gydion's eyes creased as Rose flinched, startled at his presence. "However, you are small in number and you have not yet unified the incantatio. We are with you, my friends but take care not to promise again, something that you are unable to deliver. Our memories are long and our vengeance legendary. You believe that we need you to win back this land for us. We do not. The Fae rule here now, there are no Whytes, but for you of course."

"There are more of us than you are aware Gydion," said Rose, "you may be surprised when you see them for yourself. We have formed an allegiance with the Twocasts of the Ebony Forest. Many have at least one Whyte ancestor and I do not doubt that these people are our kin. They are led by Elder, an extremely powerful Witch. She is the child of two Whyte ascendants."

"Ruzha and Sevti's child survives?" Gydion's black eyes were like bottomless pits.

"Ruzha and Sevti's child?" Rose gasped at the enormity of this revelation.

"I see you were unaware of this," said Gydion. "That a child such as this should survive for over a thousand years... You understand what this means Rose?"

Rose knew exactly what it meant; Elder was her family, and not only because she was a Whyte. No, they were related in the much more fundamental sense of the word. Now Rose understood why, from the first time she had set eyes on Elder, she had felt a connection to the woman.

"Rose, you share the same spirit vapour," Gydion spoke slowly, his words stilted as if talking to a child. "Inside this woman fractions of Ruzha and Sevti's essence live on. It is the source of her magical ability and her longevity. How powerful is Elder's magic?"

"Considerable, from what I have seen," said Rose, "why do you ask?"

"Do you know the fate that generally befalls the children of two Ascendants Rose?"

Rose shook her head. Something twisted in her stomach.

"Decapitation."

"That... that's barbaric!" Rose's hand flew to her mouth.

"It was thought to be the only way to preserve the potens," said Gydion, "Fractioned vapours are released, allowing them to flow back to their rightful Ascendant. This prevents dilution and maintains the integrity of the potens for future ascents," he hesitated. "The power of an Ascendant is compromised by the presence of living offspring. Terribly compromised... any Ascendant Rose."

He can't mean... Rose's eyes brimmed with tears as she levelled them squarely at Gydion. "What exactly are you trying to tell me Gydion?"

Vacant eyes skirted the ground before returning to confront Rose's narrowed glare.

"Rose, it is my duty to tell you that you will not possess the power required to cast the incantatio unless the Elder Witch's reign comes to a very abrupt end."

∗ ∗ ∗ ∗ ∗

Rose, haunted by Gydion's words, slept little that night. Now, as they trudged northwards along the shores of Knucker Bay and towards the Frozen Falls, her thoughts remained in turmoil. Could killing one person to save the lives of millions of innocents ever be justified? Even if it could, am I really capable of taking the life of my friend, my family, part of my very soul?

They all walked in silence, the others quickly noticing her mood as Rose set off at a pace that actively discouraged conversation. The majority of the group lagged way behind her now and even Ash struggled to keep up.

She tugged her mind from its chaotic quandary, choosing to focus her attention on the rhythmic crunch of their boots on the snow, which was bizarrely comforting though the relief was only temporary. A seabird screeched as it soared above her, climbing high into the sapphire sky and piercing her concentration, allowing her thoughts to flood back in once more, like a tsunami of pain.

Pausing, Rose closed her eyes, drawing in a long breath. The moist air tasted of salt and seaweed. It dried on her skin, leaving a fine powdery residue.

"You okay?" Ash cupped her elbow in his hand.

"No, I'm not Okay," The words were spoken so softly that she had not expected him to hear them.

She watched his angular features cloud in concern. His cheeks were crimson splotches, whipped by the brisk sea breeze. His eyebrows and the edges of his chestnut hair glistened white with salt and frost. The effect was comical and despite her melancholy, Rose could not prevent her lips from lifting.

"You look like a Twocast," she said, her grin widening, "by the time we get to Isingwilde your hair will be as white as mine."

"Don't change the subject, Rose," Ash cast a glance back to the others who were quickly gaining on them. "You've been acting strange ever since you came back from your meeting with the Fae. What did Gydion say to you, has someone died? Did they say something about Vega and the others, or Aureus? Is it Lord Dux?"

"Ash, if I knew anything like that do you really think I'd keep that from you?"

"No… I'm sorry, of course not," Ash squirmed, "but I know you… it's something awful isn't it?"

"I don't want…" Rose hesitated as Linden and the others approached them. "I can't talk about it now Ash and to be honest, I'm not sure that I'll ever be able to discuss it. Please don't press me on this."

"Alright Rose," his voice dropped to a whisper, "but remember, the tree that stands alone is destroyed by the storm while those in the forest grow taller."

"Ash? That's from Ka's Unification." Rose could not keep the note of surprise from her voice. "Have you been reading Auriel's books?"

"No, of course not," Ash flushed. "Dux made us all read it before we left, although I only got about half way through. It's really long and incredibly dull, but there are one or two quotes of his that just seem to cut right to it, you know what I mean?"

"Yes, I do," Rose knew exactly what he meant. Despite much of the bigoted rhetoric that was said to originate from Lord Ka, The Unification unveiled many truths that cried out to be told and much of the prose was remarkably moving. If only his motivations had been as pure as many of his words. If he had not ultimately been driven more by the pursuit of power, maybe they would be fighting on the same side."

"You heard it too then?" Linden approached them with his hand outstretched, gesturing beyond them to the North. "We must be getting close to the falls."

"Whatever you two were talking about must have been riveting," He met their questioning looks with a wry smile, "if you failed to hear that."

Having grown accustomed to the rhythmical pounding of the ocean as they journeyed along the shoreline, Rose hadn't noticed the distant hissing rumble. The alternating hiss of the ebbing and flowing waves had been replaced by a constant, pounding roar.

"I thought that the Frozen Falls were…well… frozen," Said Ash, "so how come they're making so much noise?"

"They're only completely frozen in the winter," said Auriel, breathlessly as she took the last few steps towards them up the incline. "In the spring, the central channel thaws but the majority of the falls stay frozen right the way through summer."

"How big are they?" asked Ash.

"About five hundred feet wide and two hundred high, the source of the water is the glacier way up in the centre of the Ice Mountains," Auriel said, expertly extracting the relevant information from the collection of encyclopaedias that was her memory.

"Jeez," Ash scratched his head, dislodging some of the snow that had collected in his hair as he did so. He let out a shrill whistle through clenched teeth. "You know how much I hate reading Auriel, but I have to admit, you Memorix do get to learn about some fascinating stuff."

"Maybe you should take it up," said Lee, "Remember what Lady Tesler said, words are more powerful even than magic."

"Yeah, well when faced with a Djinn, I know which I'd rather rely on," Ash scoffed, "I doubt that words would be of much use then."

"The power of words is constantly underestimated," Auriel raised her chin, her jaw tightening. The merest hint of a frown creased her brow, "with words you can injure or heal, create or destroy. Words justify our existence and define our character. Even magic is useless without words."

"Don't be too hard on Ash," Rose put out her hand to assist Auriel to the summit of the slippery incline. "I don't think he's grasped the synergy of the cell system yet."

"Synergy?" Ash raised a brow.

"We are Ascendants," said Lee, "we ascend four to a cell each one of us possessing a key magical potens. Yet we each have the capability to utilise all of those potens, but whenever we act together, our powers are magnified many times. We are more than the sum of our individual potens."

"I, for one, do not believe that this design is by chance," said Rose, "because it means that none of us is indispensable."

"Except, our cell is unlike any other," said Ash, "because you are not dispensable Rose. Without you we cannot function, without you, we would not be here. We would have ascended with four of our own cast like every other Ascendant throughout history."

"That may, or may not be the case." Rose shrugged her shoulders, "I remain to be convinced of my own worth above anyone else, but either way, discussing it gets us nowhere and we need to arrive at the falls before dark."

Turning, Rose strode away without looking back.

Ash and Auriel exchanged a glance.

"I know," said Ash, "there's something wrong isn't there?"

- CHAPTER ELEVEN -

THE FROZEN FALLS

Icy crystals peppered the horse's mane, its muzzle and the hair on its flanks. El-on-ah had driven him hard and the animal's sweat and frothy breath had frozen rapidly in the air. Numerous globules of spittle adorned the beasts black coat, glistening like jewels. El-on-ah dismounted at the top of the falls, her ears deafened by the roar of hundreds of tonnes of water crashing down into the ravine below. She could feel the ground vibrating under her feet. The falls should be frozen solid. Spring has come early this year.

The plummeting water released a freezing spray. Whipped up by the wind, the icy mist stung her eyes and lashed into her skin, burning it crimson. Rubbing away her tears, she scanned the brim of the cliff for the track leading down to the base of the falls. When she saw it, she knew that she could not risk descending on horseback. She would have to make her way down on foot.

El-on-ah unrolled the thick blanket hitched to her saddle and tossed it over the horse's shoulders and rump, towelling him down briefly as she secured the coverlet about him. She hadn't realised how much she hated the cold until now. Why Lord Ka had ever wanted to take Rhodium from the Whytes was beyond her. They were welcome to it. Who else would want to live in this bitter, inhospitable land?

Her eyes were drawn to the southern horizon and again, she wished that Ka had allowed Puk to accompany her. She knew why he had not, Puk was his insurance, he did not trust her and maybe he was right not to. Puk would have hated the cold anyway. Still, she would prefer not to be alone when facing Knuckers and Fae. So far, she had been fortunate enough not to meet either of them.

Strapping her occultus around her shoulders and chest, El-on-ah lifted its flap and pulled out the tattered parchment that Lord Ka had given her. Only one item remained, and then this particular ordeal would be over.

It was as El-on-ah began her descent that she heard them. Faint, cheery voices drifting through the air, rising sporadically above the noise of the falls. She recognised them instantly, her heart pounding in her chest as a flurry of surprise and excitement shot through her. Wrapping her cloak around her, she crouched down and edged out towards the rim of the cliff top. Below, Rose the Whyte was approaching the base of the falls with Ash, Auriel and Lee. A giant of a Lignum Vitae officer accompanied them and he had an animal with him. It was a large white snow leopard.

El-on-ah bit down on her lip. *Isn't this exactly what I'd hoped for? The opportunity to save millions of lives, to end it all now. Just one spell and it will all be over.*

Yet El-on-ah's limbs were reluctant to stir. Her conviction had deserted her, leaving in its wake, a mind filled with uncertainty. This new Ka, the alliance with the Djinn, the assimilations, suddenly this new world was looking very different from the world of freedom and equality that she and the Ophites had long imagined.

El-on-ah removed her glove and looked down on the dragons eye stone, pulsating with eager energy. It goaded her. *Do it... do it!*

* * * *

"It's a rainbow made of marble," Auriel said, mesmerised by the spectacular panorama of the vast stretch of frozen water.

The Cascades had frozen into a glorious, monolithic facade. A central panel of about fifty yards had begun to thaw and its waters surged, lifting giant boulders and huge slabs of ice and tossing them like matchsticks. The powerful current launched the massive blocks over the precipice where they crashed deafeningly into the bay below.

The waters of the bay remained mostly frozen, though the chasm cut by the tumbling water's bulky cargo widened, even as they watched. On either side of the thundering, maelstrom there hung solid sheets of ice, draped majestically, like the curtains of a theatre's stage, drawn back to reveal its star performer.

"Over there," Rose gestured towards a section of the ice curtain that was silver in colour and forged into a collection of delicate glistening folds. "Fingers of silver hue?"

"Yes, undoubtedly, but how do we get to them?" Lee shielded his eyes as he looked out across the bay. "The ice is thawing, I doubt that it will hold our weight, the spring thaw is evidently well underway."

"There's a cave behind the falls," said Auriel, delving into her library of stored knowledge. "Apparently it was quite an attraction in ancient times. The Whytes used to call it The Great Ice Grotto. If the entrance is still accessible, then we should be able to collect them from inside, without even venturing out onto the ice."

"I don't see any cave entrance," said Lee, squinting, "I should refer to another volume if I were you."

"It's the definitive guide," said Auriel, "*The Geographical History of Rhodium and its Islands*. So, if it says there's a land accessible entrance here, then there is. You're just not looking hard enough."

Sloley chattered excitedly while frantically attempting to bury himself inside Lee's hood.

"Hey," Lee winced as sharp claws dug into his neck, "what's up with you? Stop being such a pain…"

"There," Linden pointed to a spot about twenty feet from where they were standing.

There, between two folds of iridescent blue ice, was a dark crevice, about the size a tree trunk. The crack, set back beyond a small ledge, rested about three feet above ground level. Effortlessly, Linden vaulted onto the outcrop. He turned and extended a hand as the snow leopard leapt up beside him.

Sloley's chattering appeared to be mounting in line with his degree of agitation. Pulling the distraught loris from his shoulder, Lee stuffed the flailing animal into his occultus and climbed up onto the ledge.

One by one, they slipped behind the ice curtain and into the hidden chamber. Inside, the giant cavern was a multi-coloured kaleidoscope of light, each fold of the curtain acting like a giant prism and splitting the sunlight into a rainbow of colours. The ice too was painted with a variety of hues, each of the minerals trapped inside bestowing a different colour. The folds seem to alter in tone as they led further into the cave and towards the centre of the falls. The ice at the entrance was blue, transforming to green and then, as the sunlight cut through it, distinct stripes could be seen, pinks, golds, purples and, deeper inside the cavern, a brilliant, gleaming silver.

"Wow," said Ash, "It's like someone stole all of Rhodium's colours and stashed them in here for posterity. I can see why this place was such an attraction with the locals. Is that what we are looking for?"

He pointed towards the silver portion of the curtain, stretching out towards the centre of the falls.

"A simple task," Linden said, striding over towards the fingers of silver ice.

He gripped one of the fingers in his gloved hand and broke it off. The action produced a loud crack which, amplified by the acoustics of the vast amphitheatre reverberated around the cavern. The vibrations seemed to grow stronger, transforming into a different sound, an expanding, rumbling, guttural roar.

The grey-scaled beast emerged from the shadows. Shielded, behind her, were two hatchlings teetering on the edge of a nest containing a collection of unhatched eggs and broken shells. The creature's yellow eyes locked onto them with the focused determination of mother protecting her young, her enormous fangs dripping with spew.

"Shit," said Linden, "here." in one smooth movement he tossed the stick of ice to Auriel and drew his sword from its sheath. The action prompted the dragon to let out an almighty roar. The beast jerked back its neck preparing to strike.

"Run!" Linden yelled as he faced off the beast, his sword levelled at the animal's soft underbelly.

The leopard sprang to Linden's side, emitting a low, menacing snarl through bared teeth. Auriel and Lee dived behind an over-sized stalagmite. The knucker's neck snapped around. A bolt of spew hit the boulder with a loud crack, freezing it instantly. The rock shuddered, emitting a growing rumble like the onset of an earthquake, shaking progressively more violently until it exploded into a million pieces.

The blast flung Auriel back against the wall of the cavern where she dropped to the ground and lay unmoving. Lee's face, now deathly pale, was peppered with tiny cuts. Crouching behind a large boulder, Lee's eyes gazed vacantly, fixed on the body of the small loris lying limp and still by his side, a large shard of rock jutting from his abdomen.

Rose glanced anxiously towards Ash. *If we do not act, it will tear us apart.* Silently she signalled her intentions. Ash nodded and they began circling around the creature, moving back towards the rear of the cave, their attention never deviating from the animal's enormous body, which now blocked their escape.

Letting out a tremendous roar, the great beast swung around, returning its attention to Linden and Ro-eh-na. Lifting its head, the animal prepared to strike. Linden raised his sword above his head, charging at the beast as it shot another jet of spew towards him. The leopard leapt onto the dragon's shoulders. Ro-en-ah tugged hard, biting deep into its neck, wrenching its enormous head back in an attempt to disrupt its aim, but she was not fast enough. The spew hit Linden's right arm, rapidly penetrating his thick bearskin coat and soaking through onto his skin.

Linden's scream was visceral. It shook the cavern, echoing around the grotto for long after his body had ceased its tortured convulsions. Finally, he lay unconscious, his right arm, blistering, blackened and frozen.

Ro-eh-na burst into a frenzy of action, attacking the beast with fangs and claws, repeatedly sinking them deep into the knucker's hide. She did little damage and with one great flick of its tail, the animal dispatched her as effortlessly as a horse dispatching a fly.

Rose's response was lightning fast. Once Ro-eh-na was safely out of the way, she took aim.

"Revincio," Rose swung her arm around in a circular movement and cast the binding spell.

A stream of white energy sprung from her potens ring and shot out towards the dragon. It snaked about the animals form, coiling around its jaws and limbs and then tightening about the animal like thick silver twine.

"It won't hold her for long," said Rose, as the dragon crashed into the walls of the cavern, thrashing and heaving its body around in an attempt to escape from the restraints. "The knucker we got the spew from must have been a juvenile. She's much bigger and stronger; I doubt a holding spell would restrain her at all."

A loud crack sounded as one strand of the magical tether snapped, releasing the dragon's wings, which flapped madly as it fought to regain an upright position.

"If she gets her jaws free she'll have us for sure," said Ash. "Maybe we should fight ice with ice…"

His words confused her momentarily, but she rapidly grasped his meaning.

"No, Ash, that's much too dangerous."

"Well, if you can think of another way…" Ash said as another tether snapped. The beast's forelegs were free. "You've got about thirty seconds."

Rose knew he was right, the spell would not hold much longer. She held his gaze for a long moment. Either way, chances were that they would both be ripped apart and Rose had no better plan. Reluctantly she nodded her approval.

Ash's transformation was almost instant, which was as well because just then, the last of the tethers fell away and the animal hurtled towards them at full speed. Knocking Rose aside, Ash charged the dragon just as it raised its head to strike. The two beasts clashed, the ground juddering violently as they thundered into one another. The creature's monstrous cries filled the cavern, loud enough to obscure the roar of the water pounding into the bay.

Though the snow leopards teeth and claws had made little impression on the hide of the Knucker, the dragon's equipment appeared to be altogether more superior. Each dragon latched on, their arched fangs ripping deeply into each other's flesh. Claws gouged deep grooves into their flanks. The floor of the grotto swam with viscous, inky blood.

Ash was becoming increasingly overpowered by the larger, more powerful beast. Rose's heart twisted in her chest. *I cannot lose him... There has to be something I can do.*

The creature shook Ash like a dog, tossing him to the ground and arching its neck ready for one final, deadly strike. Rose reacted instinctively, running forward and placing herself between the two of them. The beast hesitated for an instant as it caught sight of her diminutive figure, hand raised in challenge, eyes narrowed and awash with fury.

"You will not take him," She yelled, hesitating as she heard the muffled voices of the four, whispering to her, growing in intensity, urging her on... *Occillo? - Really? Can it be that easy? It doesn't matter, I'm out of options.* Rose cast the spell.

"Occillo!"

A bolt of magical energy surged from her ring, striking the animal in the centre of its chest. Though stunned, the beast seemed to absorb the impact with little effect, but the bolt of energy had opened up a fissure between the scales at the centre of its massive chest. Rose held her breath as the crack widened, slowly expanding until white energy flowed, tiny rivers of lava running between its scales until they were rimmed with fiery silver light. The beast swayed before her, glowing like an enchanted, three-dimensional mosaic.

Realising what was about to transpire, Rose flung herself to the ground, rolling behind a large boulder. The dragon let out a blood-curdling howl. Rose felt a deep rumble beneath her and then everything began to vibrate. Large shards of ice dropped like giant knives from the roof of the cavern, piercing the ground.

The creature's form grew blurred and indistinct, its scales vibrating like the wings of a thousand hummingbirds fighting for freedom. One broke away, flying past Rose like a leaf in a storm. One by one more followed, then small groups, until finally in one enormous explosion of light the animal fractured into a thousand pieces splattering the walls of the cavern with glassy scales dripping with blood and flesh.

The silence that followed lasted only seconds but to Rose it was as if time itself had stopped. As if someone had cast a holding spell on the scene; nothing could move and no sound escape from the resulting vacuum. Then, she got to her feet and the scene before her lurched violently into focus, the sound returning in all its ghastly splendour.

Linden cried out in agony as Ro-eh-na knelt at his side, the look of fear and helplessness on her face belied her attempts to reassure him. Ash lay bleeding, propped up against a rock. He moaned as Auriel manically tore strips from her robe to use as bandages. The horrific scene was being played out to the accompaniment of unremitting, monotonous, droning sobs, emanating from behind a large boulder at the rear of the cave.

When Rose found Lee, he appeared dazed. He rocked back and forth, arms clutched about his body, tears streaming down his face as he bent over Sloley's lifeless body.

"I'm so sorry Lee," Rose placed a hand on his shoulder.

"I couldn't help him…" Lee said flatly, "some alchemist eh?"

"Lee… you can't blame yourself. You could not have prevented this, no one could have, and you can do nothing for him now." She bent down beside him and grasping his chin, she pulled his face around, meeting his eyes, "but you can help Ash and Linden and they need you now."

Stirring from his trance, Lee glanced over to where the newly hatched dragons were squawking pathetically, open-mouthed, at the edge of their nest.

"We need to move quickly," he said, swallowing, "Knuckers share the parenting of their clutches. The male could be back at any moment."

"We'd better get on with it then," Rose gave his shoulder a reassuring squeeze. "See what you can do for Linden, he's Knucker-struck. I'll help Auriel with Ash."

Rose felt a surge of guilty relief as she looked over Ash's battered face and body. *He's a Metamorph; he will heal quickly.* She recalled how Lord Irwin, their Morphology Magister, had explained that the cells of a Metamorph had the ability to shift shape and reform. It enabled them to regenerate remarkably quickly, but as she dressed his wounds, she found her anxiety growing.

"You are going to be okay aren't you?" She eased his arm back into the sleeve of his robe.

"Me? Oh, I'll be fine, I'm indestructible," he flashed a lopsided smile. "Thanks, by the way. That was some move. Whatever made you think to use the fracture spell? I thought that was just for the incantatio… for objects I mean."

"Yes, so did I," said Rose, "Instinct maybe."

"Well, I'm glad you go with your gut Rose. Don't ever stop doing that."

"It's the four," said Auriel, looping the last of the bandages around Ash's wrist. "Lord Eldwyn killed a knucker once, it's the only successful killing ever recorded and he never told anyone how he did it. He was afraid that if it ever got out knuckers would be hunted like vermin and he did not want that to happen, he wanted to preserve them. I guess it's because Rhodium has so few native species."

"Are you able to communicate with Lord Eldwyn, Rose?" Ash asked tentatively.

"No… no, I can't." Rose hesitated, "but sometimes I think that he communicates with me. Do you feel strong enough to stand?"

Ash nodded, "I said I was indestructible, didn't I?"

Taking their hands, he allowed them to help him to his feet and over to where Lee and Ro-eh-na were busily working on Linden.

"How is he?" Rose crouched down beside them.

"I've given him a sleeping potion to ease his pain," Lee's voice was subdued, "but there is no cure for knucker strike. The poison will spread until it kills him. It is just a matter of time."

"What if we remove the limb?" Ro-eh-na's words were spoken impersonally, but her eyes revealed their cost. "Will he have a chance if you take his arm?"

"I don't know," said Lee, "there are no records of any native surviving knucker-strike. That said I'm not sure if it has ever been tried before. Auriel?"

Auriel shook her head. "There's nothing recorded in any of the material that I have read."

"I'll do it. He has nothing to lose," Ro-eh-na turned to Lee, "Do you have what we'll need to cauterise the wound?"

"I have plenty of silver nitrate," said Lee, "but are you sure that you want to do this. He is Lignum Vitae; he'll not thank you for it."

"I will not be doing it for his thanks," she said, lifting Linden's sword from his side, "I do it only to save a life that I believe is worth saving."

Ro-eh-na's stood astride Linden's body, her hands trembling as she raised the blade above her head. Auriel turned away as Ro-eh-na bought the Ferrum steel down. The blade made a soft shushing sound as it sliced through flesh and bone like scissors through paper.

"Now!" Ro-eh-na voice cracked as she choked back a sob, "Lee, do it now!"

Carefully, Lee laid the stick of silver nitrate over the amputation site, placing his hand over the wound. The dragon's eye ring glowed red and the nitrate burst into flame, flaring brightly with a loud hiss as it cauterised Linden's wound. The air became thick with the scent of burning flesh.

Ro-eh-na finished dressing Linden's wounds while the others carried Sloley outside the cavern and buried him under a pile of rocks. They stood solemnly, without speaking, grief hanging over them like a black fog. Oppressively thick, it muffled everything, all words, all thoughts and all purpose.

"I told to stop being a pain…" Lee spoke in a monotone, "that was the last thing I said to him, that he was a pain."

"He would have known that you didn't mean it," Ash winced as he put his arm around his friend's shoulder, "he was a smart little critter."

"Yes he was, but I can't help thinking that maybe he would still be here," said Lee, "if I had not tried to dive behind the boulder."

"If you hadn't, you'd probably both have been killed," Rose squeezed his hand. "You reacted the way any of us would. Sloley will always be a part of our story Lee, and we're not finished yet. We will take back our lands from Lord Ka because we cannot allow him to continue to oppress and enslave our people. When we triumph, we will remember that Sloley played a vital part in that victory. If it were not for him, we might not have found the means to unify the incantatio. His death will not have been in vain."

Later when they left the cave, Linden, heavily sedated, slept peacefully on a sledge fashioned from driftwood and lined with his thick bearskin cloak, which was wrapped tightly around him. Ro-eh-na made easy work of pulling the sleigh, the task held no challenge for the powerfully built snow leopard, even with Linden's great body cradled inside. Harnessed to the device with a yoke made from Lindens leather armour straps, she moved rapidly over the snow and frozen ground.

"I realise that we still have one final piece of the incantatio to locate," Ash fell into step beside Rose. "But with Linden... What are we going to do Rose?"

"We don't have any choice, we can't deviate from our original plan," Rose slowed as she saw Ash was limping, though he attempted to hide it. "Lord Eldwyn saw it all Ash, he predicted every move that we would make. Each piece of the puzzle has been strategically placed accordingly. Therefore, if we are to complete the Incantatio, we must stick to our planned path. We have to rendezvous with Elder and the others at Isingwilde as arranged."

Their weary legs crunched through the thick snow as they trekked onwards towards the northern Rhodium town of Isingwilde. They did not look back. They did not see the black-robed woman climb down to the base of the falls and enter the Ice Grotto. Nor did they watch as she emerged, minutes later, clutching her occultus to her as if it contained the cure for all the ills of the world.

- CHAPTER TWELVE -

ISINGWILD

As they reached the summit of the smallest peak of the Ice Mountains, Rose finally got her first view of Isingwilde. Its citadel and surrounding dwellings lay stretched out below them. Isingwilde's great Ice Castle, framed by two giant snow-covered pines, glistened in the weak evening sunlight, the spires of its five turrets rising majestically into the skyline.

The castle, its city walls, and surrounding dwellings seemed to remain virtually intact despite withstanding the ravages of War and centuries of Rhodium's devastating ice storms. Beyond the citadel, loomed a magnificent backdrop, the towering snow-covered glaciers of Knucker Island, which hung eerily on the horizon, floating on the mist that drifted over the silver waters of Knucker Bay.

"Look… look over there," Ash gestured towards the gatehouse on the eastern wall of the city where a ribbon of smoke curled lazily upwards in the still morning air. "I knew it wasn't my imagination, I did smell smoke. They made it!"

Rose did not respond. Her attention was taken by the two large sailing vessels anchored in the bay. Ash followed her gaze.

"Are those Aurum standards?" His jaw dropped open. "That must mean…"

"We cannot be sure what it means until we get down there," said Rose, tempering the small ember of hope that flickered briefly inside her. "When we left Aurum the skies were heaving with Afreet, I can't see how anyone could have escaped. We could be walking into a trap."

"Neither Ka nor the Afreet could know that we'd come here," Auriel's words were spoken so rapidly that they caught in her throat. "The ships must be from Aurum. Rose, Lord Dux, the Magisters, and the rest of the novices, they could all be alive."

"Rose is right," said Lee, effortlessly maintaining his cool. "We cannot let emotions sway us. We need to be sure that we are not walking into a trap."

"Then I'll go and make sure," said Ash, "you continue on down, and I'll fly ahead and check things out. If you wait at the foot of the valley, I'll meet you there and let you know if we have anything to fear."

"No, Metamorph or not, you are still recovering from your injuries," said Rose, "I am not happy with that plan."

"I'll take care Rose," he shot her a conspiratorial wink, "I'm indestructible remember."

"Indestructible or not," she said, "Your wounds are still not entirely healed. We remain together. It will be dark by the time we reach the foot of the mountain so no one will see us approach. We'll make our way to the eastern gatehouse as soon as it's dark. Hopefully, we can get a good look at whoever is warming their behind by that fire."

The dusk faded from purple to black as they made their way silently towards the gatehouse. A crescent moon provided scant light, though it was adequate enough for them to negotiate the rubble-strewn track leading to the city walls.

It soon became apparent that their caution had been unnecessary, and it was obvious who they would find warming his backside by the fire. The scent of wood smoke grew stronger as they neared the building. It drifted towards them in the fresh easterly breeze, and that was not all that the breeze carried.

"You can all hear that, right?" Said Ash

Their weary faces relaxed into smiles of relief as they heard the unmistakeable sound of fiddle music accompanying a male voice, singing with a broad Ferrish drawl.

'Oh now where do I be,
I be in the land of Rhodium see,
Where the winds so cold it freezes pee,
And knuckers are a roamin' free.
Oh now where do I stay,
I stay in the land where roams the Fae,
Where the fires kept burning night and day,
Else you'll freeze and die right where you lay,
So take me from this barren land,
To where the deer, the bees and the wild boar roam,
Where the sun is warm and, I was grown,
Take me back… take me back home."

"Vega!" Four voices rang out simultaneously with the Tinker's name, the melancholy and fatigue of the past day lifting as they raced towards the gatehouse. In their excitement, they had forgotten about Ro-eh-na and Linden, who followed on behind at a somewhat less frenetic pace.

They pounded on the thick wooden door of the gatehouse. It swung open almost immediately. Vega stood there, his fiddle still in his hand and his face a picture of surprise and relief.

"Well, if you ain't a sight for sore eyes," he said, "come in, come in. Lyra, look who we have here... woman o' the house, make some tea."

The short, burly tinker greeted them all with open arms, hugging each in turn.

"Rose, I knew you'd make it," Vega's arms enveloped her slim frame pulling her to him and squashing her face into his chest. "I told them, I did. I said that girl would not let little things like knuckers or Fae stop her, Lord Edlwyn knew what he was about when he sent her to us, so he did. "

Rose stiffened. Her heart heavy in her chest. Yes, we made it, but at what price? Lord Eldwyn's plans are not devoid of flaws.

"Vega, Linden has been severely wounded, he may die," said Rose, "we need to get him into the warm and he needs healing. We do not have the knowledge or the expertise to treat him."

"I'm sad to hear that," Vega caught sight of Ro-eh-na attempting to drag the heavy sledge through the doorway. "Wait, Lass, let me aid yer."

They manoeuvred the stretcher into a small room off the main living room. The bearskin covering Linden's body slipped away. Vega went to replace it, recoiling as he saw the extent of Lindens injuries.

"Knucker-strike," said Ash, "we are all lucky to be alive. If it wasn't for Rose…"

"It was a team effort," said Rose, "The fact that we did not all make it in one piece, now that is my responsibility alone, unless... Vega, why is the Aurum fleet in the harbour?"

"Ah, now there's a story you'll be happy to hear," said Vega, suddenly animated. "Lord Dux cast a shield spell on the oratory, and being the great wizard that he is, it held long enough for them all to escape through the tunnels to the port at Aurora."

"Everyone made it out of the city?" Said Ash.

"Nae, Lad. I'm afraid they didn't. Just those who were in the oratory at the time, not even Lord Dux could save the remainder of the city folk."

"I didn't know there were tunnels under the Oratory," said Auriel.

"Aye, they've been there since the Dragon Wars, there are tunnels under all the major cities. They're mostly derelict and very dangerous," said Vega, "So the Magisters keep their presence from the novices."

"Vega, I don't understand how Lord Dux would know to come here?" Said Rose, "Who could have got word to him when no one was aware that he had survived?"

"Have you forgotten about the Sooth?" said Vega.

Of course, the Sooth knew everything about everything, except the whereabouts of the incantatio.

Linden groaned as they slid his bed towards the fireplace. Though trembling with cold, his body dripped with perspiration.

"I'll send word to Lord Dux that you're here," said Vega, "Lord De Lille has many of his apothecary materials with him, and if he can't heal Linden then I doubt that anyone can. I expect Lord Dux will be impatient t' speak to yer Rose."

"Yes," Rose waivered as she attempted to hide the fury welling up inside of her. "I am eager to speak with him also."

- CHAPTER THIRTEEN -

THE SOOTH

Flanked by a battalion of Afreet and trailed by seven coaches containing his entourage, Ka's carriage entered the deserted city of Aureus. A herd of goats, disturbed by their approach darted into a small alley, their bells clanging jarringly as they disappeared from view. Ka's gaze followed a clump of hairy weeds, tumbling ahead of them in the empty roadway. Soon these roads will be lined with cheering crowds kneeling before the Ascendant, who freed them from tyranny.

Ka's eyes ate up the beauty of the city, each marble and gold clad building, every corner bringing forth a new vision for him to savour. There were ornate statues, fountains that leapt high into the air conjuring mini rainbows from the sunlight, and stores brimming with exotic foods, wines, colourful fabrics and precious jewels. It had been over a thousand years since he had last roamed these streets. Little had changed, except now they belonged to him.

The carriage rumbled to a stop in front of the Oratory. An Afreet officer pulled down the steps, and swung open the door, giving Ka a curt bow as he exited the vehicle.

"No," Ka snapped at the guards as they moved to his side, "I shall enter alone. I will return presently and until then, please ensure that everyone remains here."

He did not look back to confirm their compliance, never questioning for one moment that they would.

As he crossed the threshold of the building, a wave of pleasure surged through him. This ancient seat of power, this bastion of the social elite was now his alone to shape. His ambitions, so long in the crafting, were about to be realised. From this day, the students passing through these gates would be known as young Ophites. They would be versed in the doctrine of The Unification and become fervent followers of his teachings.

Ka took in a long breath of air. He smiled. He was on the cusp of realising his dream, a victory so close that he could taste its sweetness. The Afterlands would be transformed into the world that he had long envisaged. But first, he had one or two small irritations to deal with.

Urgently, Ka headed towards the Atrium. His head swam as he entered its great hall, his senses overpowered by the room's pungent aroma. It was just as he remembered, the heady mix of perfumes; bergamot, lemongrass and jasmine. Like entering a humid tropical garden after a rain shower. As scents often do, it brought forth an old memory, his final soothing. He was unprepared for the accompanying feeling of nostalgia. I was so naive, he thought, this world had seemed so perfect. He pushed the thought from his head. I did not come here to reminisce.

The chamber echoed with the sound of his footsteps as Ka made his way towards the impluvium and the jewelled box resting on its adjacent pedestal. Lifting its lid, he let his fingers hover over the neat rows of rings before pulling out the large band of a Blood ascendant. A ribbon of sunlight streamed down through open rooftop lighting its dragon's eye stone. He slipped the ring onto his finger, giving a brief smile of satisfaction as the gemstone flared at the touch of his skin. It glowed, burnished radiant red, embers rekindled.

The sense of relief Ka felt from this action astounded him. The sensation was of returning home, of salvaging a lost limb and regaining its control. It was the first time he had felt this way since Phlegon's assimilation. Confidently he stepped towards the impluvium, its golden liquid quivered, rippling as he approached. Ka smiled wryly, *the Sooth trembles at my presence*.

"Praeteritum podere," he cast the incantation boldly, as if in no doubt that he had the right to summon the Sooth, but, in truth, his bravado was a facade, a challenge to his contaminated body. He dared his potens not to respond.

El-on-ah's words tormented his thoughts. She had suggested that his assimilation would leave him impotent, but he need not have worried, the dragons eye stone blazed blood red. A shaft of its crimson light struck the great mirror, bringing it instantly to life. The glass transformed into a fluid, shimmering map.

"I summon yea Sooth," he said, "and bid that you provide me with the location of Rose of the Whyte."

The image of the map dissolved into a pool of molten gold twisting and swirling in three dimensions as it formed the face of the Sooth.

"The Sooth I am, the Sooth I be." The clear, distinctive voice of the Sooth rang around the auditorium. "What right have you... to question me?"

"You know well who I am," Ka scowled, "do not toy with me Sooth, or I will decant your essence into a thousand flasks and scatter them throughout these lands."

"Within the potens beneath your skin, I sense the spirit of a djinn." The Sooth continued dispassionately. "A djinn has no right to command my support. So do what you will, I have nought to report."

"Sooth, you know well who I am. I Lord Ka, blood ascendant, alchemist and leader of the Ophites have imprisoned the Djinn you sense within me, I own him. By right of my ascendancy, I order you to comply."

"Ka-ek-tal you may well be, yet who is imprisoned is not so simple to see. I have only to comply with an Ascendant's decree when I am in him and he is in me."

He had been afraid of this. The Sooth wished to examine Ka's potens and if he sensed for a second that Phlegon had retained even the merest fraction of control, he would reject Ka's request. The Sooth could not be coerced or threatened and would repudiate anyone but an ascendant. But there may be a way to deceive him yet...

For the first time since his ascendancy, over a thousand years past, Ka waded into the thick golden liquid of the impluvium. The spiced, honey scented liquid bubbled, the aroma taking him instantly back to that day when he, a young naïve blood ascendant, had stepped into the pool for the first time. He recalled his eagerness to become a part of the strange world opening up before him. It enticed him, beckoning like a cave brimming with mystery and treasure.

Sinuous tendrils leapt around Ka's frame before plunging deep into his body, mingling with his potens, appraising its power and weighing it against the essence of the Fyre Meister Phlegon.

Ka's breath stilled, his ears thumping with the sound of his heart as it pounded furiously within his chest. *I am in control, I am in control.* Silently he repeated the mantra over and over again. Ka's words did not lie, he was in control and yet each day his grip grew ever more tenuous. If the Sooth were to discover this there would be no prize for him today and no quick solution to the irritation that was Rose the Whyte.

Then it was over, the tendrils slipped out of his body and returned the waters of the impluvium with a hollow pop. The face of the Sooth reformed, swirling into being as if the writhing golden liquid had spread its legs and given birth to the face of an old man.

"The Sooth I am, as Sooth I see, who you are and who you'll be. Ascendant Blood Alchemist, Lord Ka-ek-tal by given name, and in whose being this potens remains. Make now your request and the Sooth will give reply, for a plea from an ascendant the Sooth cannot deny."

Drawing in a deep breath Ka's thin slash of a mouth twisted into a smile, his taught crimson skin contorting into a bizarre grimace, like a grotesque clown at a Ferrish circus.

"Tell me Sooth," Ka cooed, delighting in this small victory, "where I can find the Whyte Ascendant?"

The golden liquid swirled, the map reforming around him. Reflected in the mirror, Ka's body rose from its lands like some colossal, hideous monolith. Stretched out before him was the image of a frozen tundra, acres of snow and ice and beyond this, a turreted castle framed the skyline.

"O'er snow covered desert of Rhodium's land," the Sooth's voice shook the room, "in Isingwilde the Whyte doth stay. Soon to die, by her own hand, beside the waters of Knucker Bay."

Ka's smile dropped from his face. The Sooth is incapable of lying, but how can this be true? Maybe the prophecy is flawed? Ka pushed the thought from his head. No, Lord Eldwyn was too good a wizard to have made such an error, but if my position is to be secured, then the Whyte's demise must be beyond all doubt.

Ka twisted the potens ring around his finger, making the decision in an instant. When Lady El-on-ah returns, I will brew the fractionation venom. If one casting the charm enabled me to wipe out an entire population of Whytes, then a single female should give me little cause for concern.

- CHAPTER FOURTEEN -

DECEPTION

Rose thought she heard muffled voices as knocked on the door of Dux's accommodation, but only one voice answered, bidding her enter. Despite her anger, her heart leapt as she heard those familiar, dulcet tones, and then again as she caught sight of him sitting at his desk, quill in one hand and a nugget of crystallised fruit in the other.

A large fire leapt and spit in the stone hearth next to a painted wooden screen, which partitioned Dux,'s sleeping area from the rest of his quarters. The room reeked of Dux, the sugary aroma of cinnamon and freshly brewed mint tea intermingled with the stale odour of old parchment, ink and candle wax. Rose had not believed that she would ever see him again and yet here he was, sitting at his desk, in the glow of the fire and surrounded by the sweet scent confectionary as if the whole world were made of candy and spun sugar.

He smiled warmly as she approached. Rising to greet her, he placed his quill in its stand and gestured to the chair on the far side of his desk.

"Rose, my dear child," his familiar soothing tone seemed a little strained and yet still he managed to effortlessly convey both his pleasure and relief at her presence, "I cannot tell you how pleased I am that you and the others have made it here relatively safely. Please take a seat and help yourself to some refreshments. You must be ravenous after your journey."

Rose glanced down at the tray, which contained a silver teapot, two cups and a large platter overflowing with figs, dates and an assorted collection of sugar-glazed fruits.

"No," Rose's tone was much sharper than she had intended, "...thank you, Lord Dux."

Dux's brows lifted, his puzzled and faintly disparaging expression made her feel like a naughty, petulant child. Her cheeks grew warm.

"What troubles you, Rose?" Dux asked.

"Much," Rose heaved a weary sigh, "much, troubles me, Lord Dux, though 'troubled' is a vast understatement of my feelings. I am both furious and ashamed of what I have discovered about these lands and the people that rule over them. People such as you, Lord Dux. I come to you for clarity, for reassurance. Tell me that I am wrong, Lord Dux, that I am mistaken and that we have not built our world, our society, its customs and laws, on a foundation of calculated deceit."

Can I really have been so wrong about this man?

Rose hesitated "I do not want to believe that you have lied to us Lord Dux because I am not talking about small insignificant lies. Untruths that you might murmur to protect a child from a painful reality. No, I'm talking about great, big, noxious lies that once injected spread like venom poisoning the hearts and souls of our people. I yearn for you to tell me I am wrong, because if you can't..."

"Rose…" Dux narrowed his eyes; he looked pained. "I have no idea what you are referring to, in what way…"

"Our world is broken." Her voice cracked, her tone was reproachful, though she felt her rage ebb as took in his look of bewilderment. Surely, he must know. "We exist in a land of illusion where we see only what we are taught to see, and believe only that which allows us to assuage our conscience. You teach us that each cast is equal, but I've seen that they are not. You tell us that ascendants and natives are valued equally and yet they are not. We learn that our laws forbid ascendants from procreating to avoid diluting our potens, but even this is based a lie."

His eyes widened and she heard his sudden intake of breath. How could he not know?

"You taught us that our potens are comprised of magical energy," Rose said, "and the laws of physics still apply Lord Dux. Energy, in any form, is forever conserved; it cannot just evaporate into nothingness. There is no legitimate reason why ascendants should not love, marry and have children. Though their children may indeed be mortal, the potens they inherit cannot die with them. It merely returns the bodies of the original ascendants, just as the power of the four have passed into me."

"Wherever have you got all of this nonsense from Rose?" Dux gave a dismayed shake of the head. "The ascension manuscripts are clear. There is no way to restore diluted potens. A fractured potens cannot coalesce outside of the ascension chamber. This assumption is the basis of all our celibacy laws. As far as I can recall no one has ever questioned this before, these edicts are unequivocal and sacrosanct." He hesitated, his expression pensive, "and yet… as you point out, here you are…"

"Demonstrating quite indisputably how flawed your assumption is," Rose nodded gently as she watched a spark of enlightenment ignite behind his eyes. "I have spoken with the Fae and they have no illusions about what they are. The spirits of my Whyte ancestors resides within them. The indestructibility of potens energy is more than a concept to them, it is tangible, and they feel its torturing effect every day. Each of them is doomed to live on for eternity as fractured spirits, wraiths, never to find rest, never again to feel the warmth and security of a physical body. Their leader, Gydion explained all of this to me in excruciating detail."

"You conversed with the Fae?" Dux arched his brows.

"Indeed, they would do me no harm," said Rose, "they are my kin, all that remains of the Whyte ascendants of Rhodium. Each of their bodies assembled from the fragmented potens of the Whyte ascendants ravaged by Lord Ka. A thousand years have past and yet their tattered souls still roam our lands. Ka may have shattered their essences and ripped their hearts into a million pieces, but their spirits, though mangled and redistributed, remain. Each Fae is a fusion of the dismembered potens of many ascendants, in that way, they are rather similar to me."

Rose glanced down at her hands; her fingers were trembling. "We differ only, because somehow, I was able to ascend and take physical form. Lord Eldwyn must have known all of this. It is how he was able to prophesize my Ascension. Though I doubt that he understood all of the implications of bringing me here…"

Dux shuffled uneasily on his feet, raising his hands in a gesture evidently designed to underline his sincerity.

"I find it hard to believe that Lord Eldwyn could have been unaware of anything Rose," said Dux, "He was a wise and incredibly gifted wizard, in all probability the most talented ever to ascend, but I assure you, I had no knowledge of any of this."

Dux cast his eyes downwards for a second. Placing his fingers lightly on the desk. Uncharacteristically he stumbled for words. "I know it may appear that I have been less than honest with you on this and other matters, and maybe you are right to think that. Perhaps in appeasing our consciences, we unconsciously close our eyes to the many injustices of our world. I, like many Ascendants, have lived my life for many hundreds of years. Perhaps a new pair of eyes is required to see our world as it truly is."

"I not only see it, Lord Dux, but I also intend to change it," said Rose.

"Rose, the path to Erebus is scattered with objectives such as yours. Indeed, many would argue that Lord Ka's intentions were just as noble when he set out on the path ultimately leading him to commit genocide."

"I am not Lord Ka, and I am in no doubt about what needs to be done. Though sometimes I question the right I have to do it."

"Why else are you here?" Dux leant forwards and placed his hand over hers. "Rarely have I met such strength and wisdom in one so young. I have no doubt that you will do what is necessary. It is in your nature, my child."

"No Lord Dux, you are mistaken," Tears sprang to her eyes. She ripped her hand out from under his, "I assure you that it most certainly is not!"

Dux recoiled. "Rose, what is it? What are you not telling me? What else did this Gydion say to you?"

Rose leant forward over the desk, her face within a breath of his. For a moment, she struggled to find the words. They came suddenly, like a ruptured dam, its vast black waters surging out and engulfing everything in its path.

"The Elder Witch is not merely a child of two anonymous and insignificant Whyte ascendants Lord Dux; she is Ruzha and Sevti's child. The spirits contained within her are factions of those buried within me. According to Gydion, if I ever hope to defeat Lord Ka, then I will need to take those fragments back."

Rose watched the pain and compassion course through Dux's eyes through the brimming pools that were her own. However, his hesitancy in responding displayed an awkwardness that she had never witnessed in him before. *Did he think her naïve, a child who lacked the courage to do what had to be done? Maybe he was right.* Her jaw tightened. "I am not prepared to take the life of my friend Lord Dux. I am bound to her in a way that I am bound to no other; she is my family, as much a part of me as my fingers. Elder is a child born of my very essence. I will find another way."

"Then we must look for one," Dux appeared on edge, glancing briefly towards the fireplace where the flames had begun to dwindle. "However, we have little time. The Sooth not only foretold of your journey here, but he also predicted that Lord Ka would travel to Aureus. If Ka were to ask it of him, the Sooth would be bound to reveal our whereabouts and he will not hesitate to attack the moment he has the means. I gather from Vega that the incantatio is yet to complete?"

"One piece remains to be found, but as Lord Eldwyn has planned everything else so scrupulously, I have to believe it will be located in time." Rose watched as Dux lifted one of the jellied sweets from the small dish on his desk, examining it before returning it to the bowl. He did this several times. Why is he so on edge?

"I expect that everyone is rather nervous of what may lie ahead, I know I am." Said Rose, "That is why I doubt that I can provide much reassurance. However, I would like them to know that we are not alone, the Fae will fight with us. Could you arrange for me to see everyone in the great hall early tomorrow morning?"

"Indeed, my dear," said Dux, "indeed I will."

"Oh, and please Lord Dux, say nothing to Elder of our conversation. I wish to speak to her myself when the time is right."

Dux's eyes fell briefly to the ground.

"Of course, Rose," resolutely, Dux met her gaze, "I will say nothing, you have my word."

* * * * *

As the door clicked shut, a willowy figure emerged from behind the tall painted screen beside the fireplace.

"All becomes clear," A wistful glow lit the old woman's eyes. "Lord Eldwyn has to be congratulated for planning everything so meticulously. His power of reasoning and prophecy is indeed truly legendary. You realise what this means of course?"

Dux held Elder's gaze for some time though he did not answer.

- CHAPTER FIFTEEN -

REUNION

The great hall had been prepared for a celebration of their reunion. Tables were laid for a veritable feast, the wine cellar had been opened, the silver freshly polished and every fiddle tuned. Ash, Lee and Auriel entered to a round of thunderous applause, boots were stamped in accompaniment and there were whoops of delight from the children. Lord De Lille hurried over to greet them.

"Ash, Lee… all of you, we are so very glad to see you," He gripped hold of their shoulders. "Come, we have a place set for all of you on the high table," he hesitated, frowning, his eyes looking beyond them, towards the open door. "Is Lady Rose not joining us?"

"Rose is meeting with Lord Dux," said Ash, "I'm sure she'll join us when she is done."

As they made their way towards the high table, they were mobbed by members of the Twocasts and Ferrish council, who patted their shoulders, shook their hands and attempted to entice them to sit beside them. However, their primary motive was clear. "Is Lady Rose not with you?" "Will she be joining you later?" "Lady Rose, she is well?"

Ferrish music skipped through the air as they took their seats between the four Magisters and members of the Ferrish high council. Three remained unoccupied, evidently they were reserved for Elder, Rose and Lord Dux.

A huge fire blazed in the hearth behind them. Above it, turning leisurely on a spit hung an expertly butchered snow deer, which filled the room with its mouth-watering aroma. Twocast woman sliced off great hunks of meat from the animal, plating them up before setting them down on the table before them.

"Boy, I'm ready for this!" Ash cut off a chunk of meat, devouring it unceremoniously.

Lee pushed his plate aside, the joyfulness of the occasion underlining his misery.

"You should eat something," said Auriel softly, "you've not eaten since…"

"I know," said Lee, "I cannot… Not yet."

"You know," said Ash, preparing to refill his mouth, "for a member of a cast with no emotions …"

"Shut up Ash! …I miss him okay, and right now, I don't think I could eat a thing without throwing up. So leave me be."

"Sure," Ash flushed. He laid his hand gently on Lee's shoulder, "but, Auriel's right, you need to eat. We all miss Sloley, but maybe everyone would feel better if we tried celebrating his life, rather than mourning his death. Without him, we may not have even made it here. Sloley would not want you to suffer like this."

"Ash is right," said Auriel, "you do not honour Sloley's life by destroying your own." She slid his plate back towards him across the table. "Please…"

After a few seconds, Lee took his fork and speared a small piece of meat, forcing it into his mouth.

"Ouch," Auriel rubbed her arm where Ash had nudged her with his elbow. "You really don't know your own strength do you?"

"Look over there," Ash cast his eyes towards a table to the right of theirs. "Do you see what I see?"

Che and Tu-nek-ta seemed to be enjoying a joke with a table full of Twocasts.

"So?" Auriel shrugged.

"He means they are no longer under the effects of the oblitus potion," said Lee, "you can tell by their eyes."

"Is that wise?" Auriel's eyes widened, "I thought the whole point of using the oblitus was to prevent them from getting word to El-on-ah about our whereabouts. They could put all of..."

"I assure you that they can be trusted," Lord Elm interrupted, "they have been living and working with the Twocasts since we left the Ebony Forest and they've grown close to them, especially the children. Then when they heard what Rose believed about the cast system, particularly her assertion that Lords and Ladies were no better than any native, they decided to join us. Few of us have any doubts about their loyalty now."

"Well let's hope you're right," said Ash

"So where is Lady Rose?" Hazel leant across the table, nonchalantly waving an empty wine glass in their faces. "Is she not aware that her minions are impatient to hear of her adventures and of her plans of course?"

A young Twocast girl appeared from nowhere and mutely refilled her goblet.

"Rose is with Lord Dux," said Lord Elm, "I expect they have much to discuss."

"You are mistaken," Hazel waved her goblet towards the large oak door at the entrance of the hall, "unless she is proficient in casting invisibility charms."

Lord Dux stood in the doorway conversing with the Elder Witch. Rose was not with them. He cast a brief, troubled glance in their direction before whispering a few words into Elder's ear. Taking hold of her arm, he led her through the arched doorway onto the balcony.

"Well, I expect Rose is tired after her ordeal," Lord Elm threw a sideways glance in Ash's direction, "or maybe she is preparing a speech. I am sure she will join us when she's ready. Until then Hazel, why not enjoy the festivities while we have the opportunity… dance?"

Elm offered a hand, and with a chuckle of surprise, Hazel allowed herself to be lead onto the dance floor.

"Ash, what is it?" Said Auriel, "You look like you've seen a knucker."

"Something is definitely not right. Rose has not been the same since she met with the Fae. Ever since then she's been acting weird... distant, and when she found out that Dux was here, well, there is no other way to describe it - she was furious. Now, after their meeting, Rose is missing, and Dux appears to be avoiding us. I have a bad feeling about all this."

"You think Rose is keeping something from us?"

"I'm certain of it and knowing Rose, there is probably something dreadfully perilous that needs doing and, naturally, she intends to deal with it without our help."

"It does seem to be becoming rather of a habit of hers," said Lee, "maybe one of us should stick close to her until we find out what is going on."

"Yes, my friend," Ash's gaze rested unwaveringly on the moonlit silhouettes of two figures conversing on the balcony. "I believe one of us should."

- CHAPTER SIXTEEN -

SACRIFICE

Rose chose not to attend the reunion. Instead, she retired early without supper. She was not yet ready to face Elder and this way, Rose could avoid the questions that she was sure would come.

Her body ached with fatigue and her brain was so weary that it resisted every attempt at reasonable thought, and yet sleep continued to elude her. This could have been due to the loud, bizarrely cheerful Ferrish music and bawdy laughter coming from the great hall, but it was not. Rose's insomnia was driven by a myriad of conflicting thoughts that infiltrated her consciousness and wrestled for dominance like sparring gladiators. *Which will be the victor? Which will be slain?*

Finally, she dozed, only to be jolted awake a few hours later, roused by the screech of a snow owl returning replete from its hunt in the early hours of the morning.

At first, Rose thought she was dreaming. The walls of her room glinted with dappled, coloured lights. Flickers of pale green, pink, yellow, blue and violet danced on the ceiling, across the walls and over her bedcovers. Slipping from her bed, Rose moved quickly to the window. The dark purple sky was awash with blinking clouds of painted light, streamers, arcs, rippling curtains and shooting rays that filled the night with colour.

A figure caught her attention. The slender woman, tall and statuesque, strolled along the shoreline of Knucker Bay. As Rose watched, the woman stepped out onto a rocky outcrop and lingered, gazing out towards the horizon. A burst of yellow light erupted from the flashing clouds, glimmering intensely. It was as if the night had pulled back its curtain and stolen an illicit glimpse of the morning sun.

Elder turned and looked back towards the castle as if she could sense Rose's eyes upon her.

Grabbing her robe and boots Rose was out of the castle in seconds. She raced towards the Bay, her heart pounding and her breath burning her throat as she sucked in the bitterly cold air. Frost collected on her lashes, weighing them down and blurring her vision. She ran on, rubbing her eyes and squinting as she searched the horizon for Elder's slender frame.

What can Elder be doing here at this hour, all alone in the darkness? Rose's breath caught in her throat. She knows... Damn Lord Dux. Now she understood why Elder had come here. Rose could not have been more certain if the words had been written in the sky.

As Rose neared the shoreline, her pace slowed as she watched the old woman teetering precariously on the edge of the rocky islet, now separated from the shore by the incoming tide. Elder's face was tilted upwards as she gazed at the restless sky, churning and iridescent with spattered colour.

The tide had turned. Waves pounded against the rocks, spray flew skywards, veiling their bodies in a fine salty mist. Rose waited silently, intent on catching her breath before announcing her presence, but she had no need. Elder new she was there.

"The lights of the northern hemisphere... wondrous aren't they?" Elder's lilt was melancholy. "They're called *Illucescente Aquilonem*, which means 'dawn of the north'. Legend has it that its presence is a harbinger of war. It would be difficult to dismiss its significance at this time, all things considered."

Elder attempted to stand, she swayed, unsteady on her feet. Grasping tightly to her staff, she turned to meet Rose's gaze with clouded, weary eyes.

"If you are here to stop me, Rose, you are too late," Elder shivered. Feebly, she attempted to pull her cloak about her. "I've taken wolfsbane, enough to kill a whole pack of Rougarou. You could not help me now, even if I wished it."

Tears sprang to Rose's eyes. She fell to her knees on the shore, the waves soaking her robe. Yet the bite of the freezing water was nothing, compared to the grief that pierced her heart.

"Why? - We... could... have found... another... way..." Rose struggled to contain her sobs. "You are my family... I... need... you."

"My dear Rose." Struggling to raise her words over the hissing ocean, Elder staggered forwards, dropping onto a large flat-topped rock where she reclined, smiling as she looked into Rose's eyes. "Soon, there will be no discerning where I finish and you begin. We will be as one; your strength will grow beyond all imagination. Everything will be as Lord Eldwyn intended, just as he planned for you to have this."

Elder fought to take a breath and then, summoning all of her strength, she swung her staff above her head, bringing it crashing down. It's knotted, carved head smashed against the rocks releasing the vermarine crystal set into its hilt. Lifting the pulsating emerald orb from the ground, Elder tossed it towards Rose where it fell with a soft crunch at her feet.

"Lord Eldwyn left that for me when I was just a few weeks old, days later he and all of the Whytes, including my mother and father, had gone forever. When I was older, I was told that the stone was a gift from my parents. It became a source of great comfort to me then because, in spite of my abandonment, it allowed me to believe that my parents had loved me. Why else would they bequeath me such a precious gift? Now I know... it was a gift meant only for you Rose the Whyte."

Rose took the pulsating crystal into her hand. Its glow intensified, lighting her face, illuminating the tracks of her tears, flickering silver, then green - silver - green - silver...

"Rose?" Elder's voice was tinged with panic, her eyes staring vacantly into the darkness. "Rose, I can no longer see your face. The night blackens around me, its stars snuffed out; its moon no longer casts its shadows. Rose, I have lived for over one hundred lifetimes, I have seen countless lives born into this world and I have watched those same lives shrivel and die. Death is an old acquaintance of mine and yet, I am afraid..."

Dropping the shining orb to the ground Rose strode out into the waves, pressing on as each surge knocked her backwards, her wet robes clinging to her small frame and dragging her down. Grasping the rocks, she hauled herself up beside the old woman, embracing her, Elder's head resting lightly on her shoulder, like that of a sleeping child.

"I'm here Elder... I'm here," said Rose. "I will not desert you, I will never ..."

"You and I," Elder's body relaxed in Rose's arms. She spoke breathlessly, "together, we will make a formidable opponent. This was the only way. Now you will earn your ryte of passage Rose of the Whyte. Take care of our people..."

"I will," Rose said, "I swear... all of them."

Elder let out a soft sigh as her body shuddered. Through misty eyes, Rose watched as Elder's chest heaved one final time and then finally stilled. She was alone, lost in a vacuum, the world silent, but for the endless crashing of the waves and a faint, distant buzzing.

Rose looked down at the frail old woman wrapped in her arms. Elder's body had taken on a strange throbbing glow and now Rose could feel vibrations as she held her, growing stronger and shaking her grip. Unnerved, she lowered Elder gently onto the boulder and backed away as the humming grew increasingly louder, becoming almost unbearable. The glowing radiance emanating from Elder's body intensified, blinding her. Rose squeezed her eyes tightly closed and covered her ears, just as the whole world exploded.

Elder's body soared into the air, rising on a torrent of energy, its force flinging Rose back against the rocks. A thousand fiery ribbons of light streamed out from Elders body and the clamour of a million hornets stung Rose's ears. Her screams were swallowed up, engulfed by the swirling maelstrom.

Elders body burst into light, releasing a pulse of energy that flew through the air like a lightning bolt. It flung Rose backwards, carrying her across the waves, over the frozen shore and beyond, burying her deep in the snow where she lay, engulfed in frosty silence.

*   *   *   *   *

"Rose… Rose, are you alright?" Hurriedly, Ash brushed the snow from her face and pulled her to him. "Rose... Please be okay… please be okay…"

Her moan drew a long sigh from his body, followed by an incongruous snigger.

"Hey Rose, you had me going then…" He forced a grin. "Promise you'll never do that again eh?"

Her eyes flickered open.

"Rose, are you okay?" Ash brushed a tendril of hair from her eyes, "if you are okay, can you please tell me what just happened?"

Rose stared blankly past him and towards the empty shoreline. *Elder?* She attempted to rise.

"Hold on now, take it steady," said Ash, "let me help you."

"I must go; I've got to ch..." Rose grasped Ash's arm.

"Okay, okay, just lean on me and steer me where you want to go," Ash pulled Rose to her feet.

They stumbled back along the bay. Elder's body was nowhere to be seen, though her robe remained, buoyed along by each lapping wave it travelled slowly up the tide line.

A few feet ahead of them, Elder's green gemstone gleamed in the frost-covered sand.

"Is that?" Ash said.

"The last piece of the incantatio," Rose retrieved the glowing crystal, clutching it to her chest. "Eldwyn concealed it within a green mineral to disguise its presence. He had everything all worked out..."

Rose turned to look at him, her eyes brimming.

"Rose?" Tilting her chin gently with his fingers, his eyes met hers. "Everything is going to be alright now. You've found the last piece of the puzzle. Isn't that what all this has been about?"

Rose caught the tremble in his voice as he spoke to her, she felt his breath on her skin and saw a familiar emotion laid bare his eyes. *I remember that look so well, and the way it feels...* Rose slipped her hand into his.

"You're smiling," he said, confused.

"I know,"

"You look weird,"

"I feel weird - Kiss me, Ash,"

He hesitated. "Now you are acting weird."

"I know," she said, "So... join me?"

"Rose, what's happened to you?"

"I've grown a thousand years Ash, and I remember things, glorious things. I just want to see if I've remembered correctly that's all."

She moved forward. "Now kiss me."

Tentatively he pulled her to him, brushing his lips lightly against her forehead. She lifted her face to his.

"No… I mean *really* kiss me."

"But Rose, we can't…"

"We could both be gone tomorrow along with everyone else, nothing left of any of us but floating wisps of vapour. Of course, if you don't want to kiss me…"

Ash brought his lips down onto hers as the Aurora intensified, its lights dancing around them, filling the sky with bursts of crimson, yellow and blue. The vermarine crystal glowed, pulsating between them as the world condensed and held only them. Their lips combined for what seemed an eternity until it ended, suddenly, in one yawning, breathless gasp.

"Was that?" Ash flushed.

"Exactly as I remembered."

"And what else do you remember Rose?"

"A life I've never lived, people I've never known and a world that no longer exists. All of them crammed into my head like a library full of picture books."

Rose turned to look out over the bay, its waters speckled with dappled hues, reflections of the kaleidoscope of colour shimmering in the night sky. Her eyes fell on the spot where Elder had given her life.

"No one could have loved their people more than she had," Rose watched as Elders robe was pushed steadily along the shore by the relentless rhythm of the tide. "She gave her life so that I would have the power to save our people, but she passed on so much more than just her potens. Ash, you have no idea. We have so much to live for... so much to lose."

Ash unlatched his cloak, wrapping it around her shoulders where he let his arm linger as they watched the reflection of the northern lights dance upon the ocean.

"Then we must win," His lips brushed her hair. "I wouldn't bet against us..."

"How very touching," El-on-ah's words startled them both. She stood behind them on a mound of sand and snow, arm outstretched, poised to strike. "Step away from her Ash."

"That is not going to happen El-on-ah." Ash turned and stepped forward, shielding Rose with his body. "You'll have to go through me first."

"One descent spell will do for the both of you when you are standing so close together, you must know that Ash. However, I would prefer not to despatch another innocent. So, step aside please Ash."

"Do as she asks Ash," said Rose, attempting to move out from behind him. She would not have him die for her.

"Oh no, you don't..." Ash grabbed her, forcing her back under his protection. "El-on-ah, think about it. If you take Rose and leave me, what do you imagine my next move will be?"

"Well if you put it that way... *Interficio*,"

A stream of crimson light leapt from El-on-ah's ring and shot towards them.

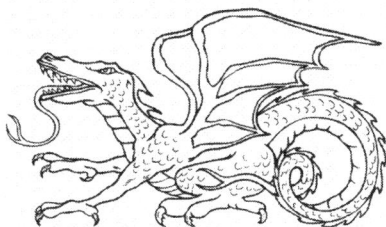

I hope that you
enjoyed reading these —

If you would be interested
in joining my 'Street Team'
of Beta readers / reviewers
drop me a line at
karenswrighton@gmail.com
and I'll add you to my
list for an arc of
    Ice and Fyre!
All the best.
    Karen . X

Proof

Made in the USA
Charleston, SC
04 May 2016